Wow. Just...*wow*.

By some unknown process which defied medical principles blood rushed simultaneously to Drew's head and down to another part of his body that he'd been trying to ignore for the last two weeks. Sophie had pulled out all of the stops this time, and the transformation made him want to fall to his knees.

She glittered...no, shimmered...in a dark blue sequinned dress which clung to her curves. High silver sandals made her legs look impossibly long, and she held a small silver and blue clutch bag. Her hair was done in a gravity-defying arrangement of curls which framed her face perfectly.

'You look...' Words failed him.

She smiled, and a bright shiver ran down his spine. 'Is that *good* speechless or *bad* speechless?'

'Good. Definitely good speechless.' Confounded as he was by her magic, Drew still couldn't quite square the mathematics of six boxes and only one dress. 'So what did your fairy godmother put in the other boxes?'

'I had a choice of dresses.' She giggled at his obvious confusion. 'Designers lend things out all the time. It's good publicity for them if a celebrity wears their latest creation.'

A sudden desire to see her in all six was quenched by the thought that she looked just perfect and he wouldn't change a thing. He rose, pulling his jacket on and she smiled, looking him up and down unashamedly.

'You scrub up pretty well too, Dr Taylor.'

Dear Reader,

There are times when being a writer gives me the opportunity to have a great deal of fun. Sophie Warner's part in a film set in the 1940s meant I needed to know something about the costumes she might wear. And how better to find out than to ask two ladies whose memories stretch way back? I owe a big thank-you to Joan and Betty, who told me everything I needed to know—along with some funny stories that I don't dare repeat! Thanks also to Lynne, for bringing both laughter and cake.

It makes me smile just to think of that morning. As I wrote this book I came to understand how much I define myself by the things I remember. Sophie's traumatic brain injury has deprived her of the ability to retain all her memories. Some aren't important, but what happens when you can't remember the name of the man you might be falling in love with? And how can she defend herself when she doesn't remember those compromising pictures on the internet ever being taken?

It's not easy for Drew Taylor, either. A love affair is all about memories—the first time you kissed, that first touch. He's not sure how he would cope if Sophie were to wake in the morning with no idea of what had happened the night before.

Thank you for reading Drew and Sophie's story. I always enjoy hearing from readers, and you can contact me via my website at annieclaydon.com

Annie x

THE DOCTOR SHE'D NEVER FORGET

BY

ANNIE CLAYDON

This is a work of fiction. Names, characters, places, locations and incidents are purely fictional and bear no relationship to any real life individuals, living or dead, or to any actual places, business establishments, locations, events or incidents. Any resemblance is entirely coincidental.

First published in Great Britain 2015
by Mills & Boon, an imprint of Harlequin (UK) Limited,
Eton House, 18-24 Paradise Road, Richmond, Surrey, TW9 1SR

ISBN: 978-0-263-25883-7

e natural,
grown in
esses conform
origin.

Cursed from an early age with a poor sense of direction and a propensity to read, **Annie Claydon** spent much of her childhood lost in books. After completing her degree in English Literature she indulged her love of romantic fiction and spent a long, hot summer writing a book of her own. It was duly rejected and life took over. A series of U-turns led in the unlikely direction of a career in computing and information technology, but the lure of the printed page proved too much to bear and she now has the perfect outlet for the stories which have always run through her head: writing Medical Romance™ for Mills & Boon®. Living in London—a city where getting lost can be a joy—she has no regrets for having taken her time in working her way back to the place that she started from.

Books by Annie Claydon

Mills & Boon® Medical Romance™

Snowbound with the Surgeon
A Doctor to Heal Her Heart
200 Harley Street: The Enigmatic Surgeon
Once Upon a Christmas Night...
Re-awakening His Shy Nurse
The Rebel and Miss Jones
The Doctor Meets Her Match
Doctor on Her Doorstep
All She Wants For Christmas
Daring to Date Her Ex

Visit the author profile page at millsandboon.co.uk for more titles

To my dear friend Betty

Praise for
Annie Claydon

'A compelling, emotional and highly poignant read that I couldn't bear to put down. Rich in pathos, humour and dramatic intensity, it's a spellbinding tale about healing old wounds, having the courage to listen to your heart and the power of love that kept me enthralled from beginning to end.'

—*GoodReads* on
Once Upon a Christmas Night...

'A lovely story—I really enjoyed this book, which was well-written by Annie, as always.'

—*GoodReads* on
Re-awakening His Shy Nurse

'Well-written, brilliant characters—I have never been disappointed by a book written by Annie Claydon.'

—*GoodReads* on
The Rebel and Miss Jones

CHAPTER ONE

FIVE MILES FELT a lot further than it had used to. The final hundred yards of Drew Taylor's morning run left him feeling dizzy and sick from exertion.

'Morning.'

If he hadn't been so keen to gulp down a pint of water and collapse into a chair, Drew would have noticed the canary-yellow sports car parked across the street from his house and reckoned that Charlie would be around somewhere. As it was, the voice behind him came as a surprise.

'Morning…' Now that he'd reached his destination, Drew's body gave up and bent double, his lungs craving air.

'You're out of shape, old man.'

'Very probably. Is that what you came to tell me?' Drew gripped his knees, staring hard at the paving stones at his feet, gasping for air.

'Nah.' Charlie shrugged and waited until Drew had recovered sufficiently to let them into the house. 'I have a proposition for you.'

Charlie's propositions were liable to get him into trouble. Their friendship had lasted since their university days on the basis that Drew was choosy about which of them he took seriously. 'What?'

'Hydrate first. You look as if you need it.'

'That sounds ominous.'

'Nah. This one's a stroke of genius.'

'Yeah. They always are.' Drew poured himself a glass of water, while Charlie flipped open the kitchen cupboard, looking for coffee.

'You've only got one coffee pod left.'

Drew shrugged. 'Take it. I'm not drinking coffee at the moment.'

Charlie twisted the edges of his mouth down, and put the pod into the machine. 'Not sleeping?'

'I'm not used to doing nothing…' Drew took a mouthful of water. That was only half the story and they both knew it.

It was his own stupid fault that he was stuck at home with nothing to do. When the hospital he'd worked in—actually lived for—had first been threatened with closure, Drew had spearheaded the campaign to keep it open. It had been a two-year struggle, culminating in failure and defeat.

When he'd finally faced the inevitable, and begun to look for another job, he'd landed one with relative ease. Head of a new memory clinic in London, which was due to open in three months' time. In any other circumstances it would have been the job that Drew's dreams were made of but now it was tainted by loss, and he was having difficulty working up much enthusiasm for it.

'You'll be thanking me in a minute, then.' Charlie smiled beatifically.

Drew gave up. When Charlie got hold of an idea, he didn't let go. They weren't always good ideas, but enough of them had been great to make his friend a millionaire before his thirtieth birthday.

'Okay. What am I going to be thanking you for?'

'Someone I know has asked me for a favour, and I think it could work out perfectly for you. It's a job…'

'I have a job, remember?'

'This is temporary. It's a fantastic opportunity to get away from it all, take a bit of a break. Two weeks, a month tops…' Charlie stopped, pressing his lips together. 'This is absolutely top secret. Totally confidential and between ourselves.'

Generally Charlie's idea of confidential was that it didn't get as far as the newspapers quite yet, but it appeared this really was a secret. Drew chuckled. 'Understood.'

'Okay. Well, you've heard of Sophie Warner?'

Drew thought for a moment. The name rang a bell, but he couldn't place it. 'I don't think so.'

Charlie rolled his eyes. 'She's a big star. Gorgeous. Didn't you see *MacAdam* on TV?'

'I doubt it. Look, I'll take it as read. Sophie Warner, brightest star in the firmament. What's that got to do with me?'

'Well, a friend of mine from America has contacted me. Carly's an assistant director and she's known Sophie Warner for years, since before she was famous. The two of them are working on a film together down in Devon at the moment.'

Friends of friends of friends. In Charlie's world it was all about who you knew, not what you knew. Drew bit back the comment, reckoning that Charlie would get to the point quicker if he didn't interrupt.

'So they did the first lot of filming over here last winter. Just caught that heavy fall of snow we had, which was a bonus, and everything went like clockwork. Now they're back again to do the summer scenes, and they've run into trouble.'

'What kind of trouble?' Drew couldn't think of anything that his particular skills might help with on a film set. Apart from an outbreak of food poisoning, and a local doctor could deal with that.

'There's something the matter with Sophie. She's acting like a diva—tantrums on set, turning up late, not learning her lines. She's had a load of bad press in the last couple of months…' Charlie shook his head. 'We won't go into that.'

It must be very bad if Charlie's sense of discretion had kicked in. The woman sounded like a nightmare. 'And what's that got to do with me? I'm a neurologist, not a minder for spoilt children.'

'That's just the thing. Carly knows Sophie and she swears that this is not just the usual film star bad behaviour. She's sticking her neck out here, and putting her own job on the line to protect Sophie, because she thinks there's something wrong with her.'

'What sort of something?'

Charlie rolled his eyes. 'If we knew that, we wouldn't ask you, would we? Apparently Sophie was in a car accident a few months back and she just hasn't been right since. She's been shutting herself away for days, running off no one knows where. You get the picture...'

The picture was becoming horribly clear. 'And your friend wants me to go down there and examine an errant film star, to see if I can come up with some medical excuse for her bad behaviour?'

'No.' Drew heaved a sigh of relief. 'Carly's already tried to get Sophie to go to a doctor and she won't have any of it. Sophie's playing a doctor in this film and so Carly wants to take you on as a set medical advisor. So you can watch Sophie and see if there really is anything wrong with her.'

'What? You *have* to be joking...' Drew drained his glass, setting it down on the kitchen counter with a crack. 'I can't do that, Charlie. It's an ethical minefield.'

'No, it's not. I've seen you step into situations before without being asked. What about that time you bundled my gran into the car and took her up to the hospital?'

'She was having a series of mini-strokes, Charlie. That's completely different.'

'No, it's not. You saw something that no one else could see, and you acted on it.'

'Yeah, and Doris isn't some wild child looking for excuses.'

Charlie shot Drew an outraged look. 'So it's okay if it's my gran, because nice little old ladies deserve your attention, is that it? You're far too eminent in your field to bother with people who might be a bit awkward.'

'No, of course not. You know me better than that, Charlie.'

'It'd be a challenge...'

Charlie knew exactly what buttons to press. He always had with Drew.

'Look, even if you could just talk to Carly, as a friend. Convince her to think about her own career for a moment and not let this Sophie character drag her down with her. I'd count it as a personal favour. At the very least it'll be a couple of days out of town to clear your head. And the bike could do with a bit of a run.'

The thought of garaging the car, and just getting on his motorbike and riding somewhere, anywhere, seemed suddenly like a plan to Drew. Alone, on the open road, he might just be able to leave the bitterness over a past that couldn't be changed behind him.

'All right. I'll talk to Carly.' He sighed. 'You'd better tell me whereabouts in Devon I'm supposed to be going.'

To give Charlie his due, everything had gone like clockwork. When he arrived at the comfortable country hotel, the receptionist was expecting him and directed him straight up to a sunny room, overlooking a nearby golf course.

He dropped his overnight bag on the bed. The drive down here had given him time to think. He'd seen this world, or one very like it, before. People who didn't say what they meant. People who pretended to be one thing when, in fact, they were another. Beautiful people, like Gina, who had taken a young doctor's heart and squeezed it hard until it had felt empty of anything but pain.

He was older now, and a great deal wiser. He'd talk to Charlie's friend, make her see sense and go back to London in the morning. No real need to even unpack. Drew was halfway to the bathroom when a knock sounded on the door.

'Carly DeAngelo.' A young woman with dark curls, an American accent, and a no-nonsense air held her hand out for a brief handshake. 'I really appreciate your coming all this way.'

'My pleasure.' It seemed that Charlie had already alerted Carly that he was coming and there was no need to seek her out.

'Is it okay if we get together in half an hour? I've got another meeting later on this evening.'

That would be more than enough time to take a shower and change out of his grime-stained clothes. 'That's fine. I'll meet you downstairs.'

Carly nodded. 'Ask for the Blue Room. I'll get them to bring us something to eat.'

The Blue Room turned out to be a small, private dining room, overlooking the sea. The highly polished table was set with heavy silver cutlery and Drew moved the centrepiece of dried flowers before he sat down. He had a feeling that eye-to-eye contact was going to be necessary to persuade Carly that this arrangement really was a bad idea.

'I'm afraid I'm going to have to ask you to sign this.' Carly extracted some stapled sheets of paper from a bulging portfolio she'd brought with her, and pushed them across the table towards him. 'It's a confidentiality agreement.'

That was fine. Drew didn't intend to even think about this after tonight, let alone talk about it. He picked up the pen that Carly had placed ready, and she shook her head. 'Read it first.'

Drew read the pages carefully and signed. 'Now we can talk.'

The appearance of a waiter put the moment off. Carly ignored the menu and ordered a salad, and Drew decided that he was too hungry to bother with food that could be picked at during the course of a conversation and ordered steak and chips. He wasn't considering saying much anyway. *No* just about covered it.

'Charlie's told you a bit about this.' She waited for the waiter to close the door behind himself before she spoke.

'He's told me that you're worried about your friend. That her behaviour's been erratic recently and she won't see a doctor.'

'Yeah. I'm a third assistant director here...' Drew raised a querying eyebrow, and Carly smiled. 'That sounds a bit more important than it is. I'm pretty low on the pecking order. Sophie helped me get the job and when we were over here last winter, doing the first lot of shooting, everything went really well.'

'And now you're back, things have changed?'

'Yeah. Joel, the director, knows that Sophie and I are close, and he's assigned me to her in the hope that I can get her under control a bit. But it's just impossible. The film world's a very small one, and no one's going to touch her when she's finished here if she's not careful.'

First things first. He wasn't a career consultant. 'If you think your friend is ill, then my first advice to you, or to her for that matter, is that she sees a doctor.'

'You're a doctor. If you stay here for a couple of weeks, then you'll see Sophie all the time.'

'I can't make any kind of diagnosis by just looking at someone. It doesn't work that way.'

'But you could tell me what you think. What the best way to proceed is. Charlie says you're a neurologist, you must be able to recognise the symptoms...'

'The symptoms of what?'

Carly flushed, looking down at her hands. 'Sophie was in a car accident about four months ago, when we went back to the States after we were here last winter. She hit her head, the side of her face was all bruised up...' Her hand wandered to her own temple and along the side of her jaw.

'And she saw a doctor after the accident?'

'Yes, she was taken to the hospital. They looked her over,

X-rayed her, gave her some painkillers and released her. Told her to come back again if there were any problems.'

'And did she?'

'No. She called me and said she was going away for a holiday, and she disappeared completely for a couple of weeks. When she got back she was…different. She's vague, and defensive, and… She's just not Sophie any more.'

It was obvious what Carly was thinking. Drew knew that this wouldn't be the first case of traumatic brain injury that had been overlooked in a general examination after an accident, and imagined it wouldn't be the last. If TBI *was* what they were dealing with here.

'I have to ask you this. Are you aware of her being involved with drink or drugs at all?'

Carly's mouth twisted. 'You've been reading the scandal sheets, haven't you.'

'No. I'd ask that question of anyone.' Maybe not quite anyone. Drew rejected the thought that it had been a little higher on the list than usual.

'She drinks a glass of wine with dinner sometimes, that's all. And it's not drugs.' Carly flashed him a defiant look. 'I'd know.'

'Would you?'

'I've been around this business long enough. I'm not stupid. For a start…'

Carly bent her little finger back, as if she was about to give a list of all the signs of drug abuse, and then swallowed her words as the waiter entered with their food.

'Something to drink?'

Drew was about to say no. It was early enough to eat and then get back on his bike and go—he'd be home by midnight. Then he caught sight of the tears brimming in Carly's eyes.

'A glass of house red would be great. Thanks.'

Carly nodded, and ordered the house white for herself. 'She's not using drugs. I'd swear to it. She doesn't even take painkillers when she has a headache, just shuts herself away in her trailer.'

'She has headaches?'

'Yeah. Fewer than she says, sometimes she just doesn't want to talk to anyone, but there are times when she's telling the truth.'

How was Carly so sure? Drew's experience of show business was limited to a couple of photographic shoots he'd been to with Gina, but his impression then had been that everyone treated the truth as if it was an optional extra. Gina had confirmed those suspicions herself, by lying to him with startling aptitude.

The waiter returned with their drinks, and Drew took a sip from his glass. At the back of his mind it registered that it was a very good red, and he took another swallow. 'Look, Carly…'

'Don't. Please don't tell me you can't help because I know that you can. Please…' Carly picked up her glass with a shaking hand and then put it down again and blew her nose on her napkin.

Perhaps Charlie had tipped her the wink that tears would help her case. Drew rejected the unworthy thought and apologised silently to his friend. Lying and manipulation were Gina's style, not Charlie's.

'Okay. What do you want me to do?' He could at least listen.

'I've got the okay to employ a medical consultant on set. I said that it might help Sophie and right now the director would try just about anything to get her to pull herself together.'

'I understand that she plays a doctor in the film.'

'Yes. It's set in 1944…' Carly pulled a large, spiral-bound document from her portfolio before Drew had a chance to object that he knew nothing about historical medical techniques.

'We've got this manual, written by an eminent medical

historian. That'll help you. And injuries are injuries, so you won't have any trouble talking to the special effects guys about making them look authentic.'

'But you've managed this far…?' Drew picked his knife and fork up, in a signal that none of this held any water, and he was going to eat. The knife sliced through the tender, succulent steak as if it were butter.

'We had a set consultant when we were here last winter, but we didn't reckon we needed anyone this time around because there's less medical emphasis. But when I told the director it might help Sophie, he agreed like a shot. No one cares about the cost of it, we're talking a multi-million-dollar project here.'

Drew wondered what those many millions might have done, applied a little more usefully. Kept his old hospital open maybe. 'Even assuming I take the job, I can't do what you ask, Carly. The thing that will really help Miss Warner is to see a doctor, in a professional setting.'

Carly's stricken look would have made Drew relent if he hadn't been so sure that he was right. 'Okay, then. What *does* work for you?'

'What works for me is that I go back to London in the morning. If you want set advice, you get in touch with someone who's interested in that kind of thing. And if you want advice on Miss Warner's condition, you persuade her to go and see a doctor.'

Carly thought for a moment. 'That makes sense. Now, given that Sophie's adamant that she won't see a doctor, and that I'm out of options and pretty desperate, is there anything else you can suggest?'

It was a straight question, with an easy enough answer. 'I could stay on for a day. I'd be happy to meet with Miss Warner and try to persuade her.'

'And she'll say no, and then you'll walk away. Job's done as far as you're concerned and nothing changes.' Carly's lip curled in contempt.

'That's not…' Drew swallowed his words. It was exactly how it was. He was the one engaging in half-truths and excuses, not Carly. If he didn't want this job, he should just say so.

But he couldn't. However unlikely his role here and despite the fact that it wasn't going to push the boundaries of medical science, it was somehow intriguing. Did he even have the right to call himself a doctor if he chose to turn his back now?

'If I decided to do it, and I haven't yet, there'd be conditions.'

'Fair enough. I want you to tell me how to do this, not the other way around.' Carly nodded him on, obviously aware that she'd found a chink in his armour.

'I'm not Miss Warner's doctor. I'm not going to guess at a diagnosis and I'm not going to report back to you on anything. If I have any concerns, I'll speak only to her about them and advise she gets proper medical help.'

'Just advising isn't going to get you anywhere. Do you plan on being a bit more assertive than that…?'

Carly's gaze met his and Drew held it for a moment. 'What do you think? Do I seem assertive enough to you?'

'Yeah. You do.' She stretched her hand out towards Drew. 'We have a deal, then?'

CHAPTER TWO

THE NEGOTIATIONS HADN'T quite finished there. Drew had insisted that a week was quite enough for them both to see whether or not the arrangement would work. For her part, Carly had vetoed his intention of returning to London the following day to pack for the week and suggested he let Charlie throw some things into a bag for him, for the set runners to collect. When he'd acquiesced, Carly had produced a contract, written in the dates by hand, and given it to Drew.

Armed with four hours' sleep, and the knowledge that he might well have signed away his sanity for the next week, Drew was on the bus with a sleepy film crew at six the following morning. Carly had told him to consider today as an orientation exercise, and Drew was more than content to maintain a watching brief.

'Five dollars on ten o'clock.' An American accent sounded from the seat behind him.

'I'm not taking dollars. I'll give you three quid that it's closer to eleven.' A woman's voice this time, speaking in a laughing, London drawl.

'You're on.' Silence for a moment and then a chuckle. 'C'mon, Madame Sophie. If you get outta that bed now, Dawn'll have to buy me coffee.'

'In your dreams. She'll have to disentangle herself from last night's waiter and wait for the uppers to kick in.' Dawn yawned loudly. 'It's not fair...'

'You had your eye on a night of passion with one of the waiters, did you?'

'No.' Dawn scoffed at the idea. 'If *we* turned up four hours late we'd get the sack. *She* does it, and Joel's all over her, grateful that she's made it at all.'

'She's the star. We can be replaced, she can't.'

'True enough. Though we've still careers when this job is finished. I'd like to be a fly on the wall when she tries for her next part.'

Drew stared straight in front of him. If this was true, then Sophie Warner was more of a nightmare than he'd reckoned. If not… The remote chance that Carly was right suddenly seemed worth taking. If Sophie *was* sick, and she continued to keep quiet about it, then things were only going to get worse.

The bus drew into a cluster of vehicles parked at the end of what looked like the main street of a small village.

'Looks as if you owe me that coffee, Dawn…' Drew couldn't help but look out of the window, in response to the voice behind him. 'She's here already.'

'Yeah, she's not going to be ready for a while. Look, she's on her way to her trailer. What's the betting she'll stay in there for another four hours?'

Drew saw Carly walking towards a group of trailers with another woman. Small and blonde, almost swamped in the large mackintosh she was wearing against the morning's chill air. They disappeared in between two of the vehicles and he craned his neck to see where they'd gone but he couldn't.

The set began to come alive for the day, and Drew maintained his watching brief. Before long, a concentrated buzz of movement centred around the main street of the village, which was a meticulous re-creation of wartime England. Further out, people in period costume mingled with the crew, almost as if the scene was dissolving, melting back into the present day.

From his vantage point, sitting in a fold-up chair at the edge of the activity, Drew suddenly saw a blonde head at the centre of it all, around which the whole shebang seemed suddenly to revolve. He looked at his watch. Eight-thirty. It looked as if Dawn was going to be paying for coffee today.

At lunchtime, the privileged few made for the group of trailers, and everyone else made a rush for the catering truck. Drew decided to wait until the scrum had died down a bit and flipped open the pages of his book.

'Hello.' Someone interrupted his reading, and Drew turned into the gaze of the greenest pair of eyes he'd ever seen. Shiny blonde hair, pinned in a wavy arrangement that was reminiscent of his grandmother's, but to quite a different effect. A dark skirt and a white blouse, under a lacy hand-knitted sweater.

'Sophie Warner.' She was looking at him as if he was a mere diversion, in the absence of anyone more interesting to talk to. 'You're the new medical consultant.'

Now that she wasn't half-obscured by distance and the milling entourage of people, he recognised her face from somewhere. Probably the TV, when he'd thought he'd only been half watching it. But he couldn't have been watching at all because it hadn't registered that she was gorgeous.

Drew smiled at her. Despite her obvious indifference to him, it was surprisingly easy to do. 'That's right. Drew Taylor.'

She nodded, as if there wasn't much more to say. Drew stood, and pulled an empty chair across the grass for her and she looked at it uncertainly and then sat down.

'Nice to meet you…um…'

'Drew.'

She gave a little nod. 'I'm not very good with names.'

Clearly that was an excuse. But whether it covered a lapse

in memory or profound disinterest in him, it was impossible to tell.

'Have you been watching this morning?'

'Yes.' Drew gestured to the copy of the script that Carly had supplied him with. 'You're not filming this in the same order that it's on the page, are you?'

'No, we're not. We go to one location, shoot all the scenes we need to do there, and then move on to the next.' She gave a little shrug.

'That sounds pretty confusing.'

Her mouth hardened suddenly. 'I'm a professional. It's part of the job.'

'Yes. Of course.' Drew had known that it would be difficult to get through to Sophie Warner. What he hadn't expected was that he'd want to, so very much.

'So have you worked out what the story's about yet?' The canvas chair creaked slightly as she settled back into her seat. Her face took on a look of composed interest, which gave Drew the distinct impression that she was doing exactly the same as he was, and prolonging the conversation in order to fish for information.

'Your character is Dr Jean Wilson, and you work at a hospital in a seaside town. Major Alan Richards is an engineer, working on a top-secret project, building and testing a new submarine. Dr Wilson meets Major Richards when she gets involved with treating some of the men who are injured during testing.'

'That's right. Only it's called a submersible. A submarine's usually bigger and can work on its own, but a submersible needs to have an outside supply of power and air.'

'Right. I'll remember that.'

'I suppose you must specialise in accident and emergency medicine.' She hardly even acknowledged his querying look. 'Since that's the kind of thing we're portraying in the film.'

A yes would have been enough. But if Drew wanted her to trust him, then it wasn't the way forward. 'I'm actually a neurologist, but I was a member of the hospital's trauma team. I have plenty of experience of all kinds of injuries, so I'm well qualified to advise here.'

'Neurology.' It was interesting that she picked on that one word. For a moment her composure faltered and then she shot him a smile, soft enough to break the strongest man, and clearly calculated to make Drew forget what she'd just let slip. 'It sounds important.'

'Yeah. I'm taking a break from important at the moment.'

Her face hardened suddenly and Drew regretted the words. He hadn't been thinking, and he'd let his prejudices show. That wasn't going to encourage any confidence on Sophie's part.

'Why?' She almost snapped the word at him.

'The hospital where I worked closed last month. I'm taking some time to look at my options for the future.'

'I'm sorry to hear that. It must have been a painful time for you.' Suddenly the ice cracked and the look of concern on her face seemed meltingly genuine. Drew reminded himself that Sophie was an actress. However beautiful she was, however much she made him long to make her smile, it was all an illusion.

He searched for something else to say. He didn't want to talk about the hospital or the closure, or how much it had hurt. They were real things, and they had no place here. 'Your English accent is very good.'

'I should hope so. I *am* English.' She waved away his apology. 'It's okay. A lot of people who saw me in *MacAdam* assume that I'm American.'

'The TV cop show? I saw the trailers.'

She gave him an amused look. 'Have you seen anything I've been in?'

'I...' Drew gave up the unequal struggle, remembering that his first task was to gain her trust, not impress her. 'I haven't had much time for TV recently, I've been pretty busy. Are you going to be making another series?'

'What?' Her sudden glassy-eyed look turned quickly into a frown.

'Another series.' Drew deliberately didn't proffer any more information. If she'd lost the thread of the conversation, he wanted to see if she could pick it up again, without prompting.

'How would *I* know?' She made it sound as if this was a detail that didn't warrant her attention.

'I just thought you might.'

'Well, you thought wrong.' She'd scanned his face, as if looking for clues, and then the frown gave way to a don't-mess-with-me glare. Sophie got abruptly to her feet and stalked away from him.

Drew watched her go. As soon as she'd put thirty yards between them her pace slowed a little, almost as if she'd calculated that she was now at a safe distance. Her angry movements gave way to a more graceful rhythm and Drew forced himself to forget the way her waist moved, and consider dispassionately whether she showed any signs of impaired co-ordination.

Nothing. She carried her beauty in a different way from Gina. Gina had known she was beautiful and had used it to wind Drew around her little finger, rock his world, and then smash it. But Sophie dealt her bewitching smiles carefully, playing her cards close to her chest. It occurred to Drew that it was a far more effective form of enchantment, and a great deal more dangerous.

She shouldn't have done that. Snapping at him and walking away only drew attention to the fact that her mind had suddenly blanked, right in the middle of a conversation. She should have thought of something clever to say to change the subject.

Clever was a bit beyond her at the moment. But she knew enough to know that no medical scenes this morning meant they didn't need a medical consultant, and Sophie had wanted to find out what he was really here for. And somewhere, hidden deep in those cool grey eyes, she'd found it. A spark of knowingness, as if he already knew the secret that no one else did.

'Forget it.' She muttered the words to herself, smiling grimly at the thought that forgetting came far too easily to her these days. People could, and would, suspect anything they pleased. If she didn't confirm those suspicions, they were nothing but idle speculation.

Carly was sitting on the steps leading up to the door of her trailer, basking in the midday sun. 'Where have you been, Soph?'

'I met the doctor.'

'Yeah? What's he like?'

'Good looking.' Sophie had always liked dark hair and light eyes in a man. 'Very good looking, actually. I don't think he approves of us much, though.'

'Why, because he's a doctor? Just because your father disapproves, it doesn't necessarily follow that *all* doctors disapprove.'

What followed or didn't follow was more than Sophie could think about at the moment. And she didn't want to think about her father either.

'He might just be shy. He's new here…' Carly warmed to her point.

'No. He's not shy.' Those grey eyes, the assessing gaze had been anything but that.

'Perhaps you are, then. You said he was good looking.' Carly shrugged, betraying a slight unease with the gesture.

'I don't know what he's doing here today. There's nothing medical in the script.'

'Forget it. Just sit back and enjoy the scenery.'

'You'll enjoy it with me?' If Carly was around, perhaps the effect of the doctor's all-too-knowing gaze would be diluted a little.

Carly grinned. 'Sorry. Can't help you with that. I've only

got one piece of male scenery on my mind, and he's back in the States.'

'So sweet. I'll tell Mark you said that.' Sophie smiled. Mark and Carly were solid, best friends, lovers… Just the sort of thing that she had dared to hope for with Josh. Everyone had told her that he was a risk, that he was a little more in love with her fame than he was with her, and Sophie had refused to believe it of him. But just when she'd been at her most vulnerable, Josh had dealt his most crushing blow.

Carly chuckled, opening the door of the trailer. Inside, the table was set for two, and lunch was waiting for them, the paper cups and plates of the catering truck banished in favour of china and glass. Sophie almost envied the altogether simpler life of rushing for a place in the queue, chatting with the film crew about the morning's work.

'Carly…'

'Yes?'

Wordlessly, Sophie hugged her friend. How could it be that one secret could erode almost everything between them? She missed being able to talk to Carly about everything, but even her closest friends were an unknown quantity these days. And Sophie knew that if she said anything, Carly would only tell her what she didn't want to hear, and insist she go for a check-up with a doctor.

'What's this for?' Carly was clinging to her tightly.

'Nothing. Does it have to be for something?' Sophie gave a final squeeze of her arms around Carly's shoulders and then let go. 'Come on. Let's eat.'

After the noise and chatter of the bus back to the hotel, Drew savoured the quiet of his hotel room for ten minutes, then opened his laptop and typed Sophie's name into the search engine. Maybe if he could watch a couple of episodes of *MacAdam* online, he'd get more of a feel for how Sophie had been before the accident. He wasn't convinced about that—after all she was an actress, playing a part—but he'd be damned if he'd admit to himself that he just wanted to see more of her.

It seemed that the internet knew all about Sophie. Her own website had pictures, a biography and a list of her acting roles, and Drew studied them carefully. Drama school and then some theatre work. She'd done Shakespeare, had small parts in a couple of blindingly awful films, and received critical acclaim for her last three films and for *MacAdam*. If it was even half-true, Sophie Warner wasn't all tantrums and bad behaviour.

The bad behaviour was there as well, though. When Drew clicked again, there were reports of reckless driving, an exposé by an ex-boyfriend, and a video clip of her slurring her words on a talk show. Drew watched it carefully, seeing the same look of glassy-eyed confusion on Sophie's face that he'd noticed this morning.

Drew shook his head. It could be anything. The papers interpreted it as drink or drugs, and Carly thought it was a brain injury. Either of them could be correct, and deciding which was true on the evidence he had so far was impossible.

His finger hovered over a link that mentioned scandalous photographs, then he decided that gossip and rumour weren't going to get him any further forward. He set about streaming the first episode of *MacAdam,* and within ten minutes of the opening credits he was well and truly hooked.

CHAPTER THREE

DREW HAD SPENT the whole of the previous evening with Sophie. He'd sat down to watch one episode of *MacAdam* and ended up watching four, back to back. He'd told himself it was an interesting show, with a great plot, but, in fact, it was Sophie he'd been unable to take his eyes off, and Sophie who'd inhabited his dreams, until it had been time to peel himself out of bed for another early start. This morning, it was in the large conference room at the hotel, which had been temporarily set aside as a rehearsal area.

Sophie looked different again. Different from the tough cop, with personal problems and a heart of gold that he'd watched last night. Different from the neatly dressed doctor he'd met yesterday.

Today she was the actress, dressed in an oversized sweatshirt, which fell by design from one shoulder, exposing the curve of her neck and the narrow strap of her top underneath. Her blonde hair was tied up in a messy bundle at the back of her head, a few wisps framing her face.

And she was alone. Sitting in one of the chairs that had been cleared against the wall to make some space in the centre of the room, yawning as she leafed through the pages of a small, leather-bound notebook.

The swing doors slapped closed behind Drew and she looked up. Even Sophie's frown was like a ray of sunshine, waking him instantly from the drowsy hangover of too little sleep.

'Hi.' She didn't say his name, and Drew wondered briefly whether she'd forgotten it again. After last night, when he'd thought he'd got to know her so well, it was a humbling experience.

'Morning. Are you ready to start?'

She shrugged, as if being in attendance was about all he could reasonably expect of her. 'I already know CPR.' She slipped the notebook into a large designer handbag, which lay on the seat next to her. He'd give a lot to know what that notebook contained.

He called her bluff, walking towards the dummy, which someone had arranged in a seated position, legs crossed, on one of the nearby chairs. 'The script says that you're resuscitating someone who's been knocked down in the street by a truck.'

Drew arranged the dummy on the floor, in a pose that vaguely resembled the kind of position a road-accident victim might end up in. Sophie looked at it with the bored air of a film star who had better things to do at seven o'clock in the morning.

'You're standing on the pavement, right?'

She nodded and he pointed to a spot a couple of feet away from the dummy. 'So that would be about here.'

'Yes, that's right.' When she stood, she seemed even smaller than she had yesterday, more fragile. Drew thought he saw a flash of uncertain fear in her eyes.

He needed to show her that he presented no threat. 'Okay. I'll give the signal and you just do what comes naturally. We'll work from there.' He gave her his most reassuring smile.

'All right.' She nodded quietly, and Drew took a couple of steps back, giving her some room. Then he clapped his hands to indicate the sickening thud of metal meeting flesh.

She jumped, whirling round in the direction of the

dummy, for all the world as if she'd just heard the screeching of brakes and the rending of tyres. Then she moved. Confident, assured, with the professional focus that he'd seen so many times on the faces of the people he'd worked with.

Kneeling by the dummy, she was examining it, counterfeiting perfectly the checks and precautions that a real doctor would take in this situation. Bending over the dummy's head, she tapped its face with two fingers.

'Unresponsive… Not breathing…' She muttered the words to herself, almost as if he'd walked out of the room and she was alone.

'Great. That's good.' As Drew knelt down beside her, her scent brushed against his senses. Sophie smelled like every desire he'd ever experienced.

She tipped her face up towards him and suddenly he was falling, unable to catch his breath. One of her eyes was the same gorgeous green he'd seen yesterday. The other was light brown, shot through with gold. The effect was stunning, the one irregularity in an otherwise perfect face. He was bewitched.

The doctor was staring at her, and this wasn't his suspicious, searching stare. If she had to put a name on it, she would call it…

No. She was mistaken, it was far too early in the morning for him to make a pass at her. And, in any case, he clearly disapproved of her, and she didn't like him all that much. Whatever had put that possibility into her head?

'Have I got breakfast all over my face?' She brushed one of her cheeks, wondering whether she'd had time for breakfast today.

'No. I…' He seemed to force his gaze downwards, towards the dummy that lay between them. The sudden, almost apologetic gesture sent tingles to the tips of her fingers.

'What is it?' She brushed the other cheek and then realised what he'd seen. 'This?' Sophie made the well-worn joke that she used whenever anyone noticed her eyes. Opening and closing each one in turn, she described a circle in the air with her finger, intoning a spooky melody.

He had such a nice smile. One that could get her into trouble if she wasn't very careful. 'You have heterochromia.'

'Yes. I wear a contact lens in my brown eye for filming, so it doesn't look weird.'

'It doesn't look weird. It's…' He shrugged, seemingly at a loss for words.

'I was born with it. It's just a pigmentation thing, nothing else.' Sophie was aware that heterochromia could sometimes be the result of an injury, and she didn't want him getting the wrong idea.

'It's beautiful.' Clearly his mind was on the aesthetics, rather than any medical implications.

Suddenly, even though neither of them was moving, the space between them seemed to close. As if all the air were being sucked out of the room, and they were being forced together by some trick of physics.

Then the vortex seemed to throw itself into reverse, and he drew back. 'The patient's probably dead by now.' He gave a regretful twist of his mouth, and Sophie's heart lurched.

'No one ever dies in a film unless the script says so. We'll perform a medical miracle.'

'Be my guest.' He sat back onto his heels, waiting for her to make the next move.

Suddenly she felt strong. She knew exactly what to do next. 'Thirty compressions and two breaths?'

'That's right.'

'But I have a second qualified person available.' She took the risk of testing her recall a little further.

'In which case?'

'One delivers compressions and the other rescue breaths. We switch every two minutes or so to avoid getting tired.'

He grinned. 'So we'll take it from the top, then?'

Sophie took a breath. Yes. It all came to her, like a well-understood routine. She checked for a response again, coming to the same conclusion as she had before. He helped her position the dummy, and she tilted its head back, ready to deliver rescue breaths.

'You start with the compressions.'

He nodded, doing as she'd told him, counting aloud when he got to twenty-five. She gave the rescue breaths right on cue, and he nodded his approval, starting the compressions again straight away.

'Do you want to try a switch?' He was concentrating on what he was doing and didn't look up at her.

'Sure. On your signal.'

The switch was perfect. Almost without thinking, Sophie fell into the lifesaving rhythm, picking up the compressions where he'd left off, using her body weight to help give her the amount of pressure that the doctor had applied. They carried on for five repeats and then switched back again.

'Perfect.' He finally sat back on his heels.

'Not so bad for an airhead, you mean?' She gave a half-smile to indicate that he could take that as a joke, if he chose.

'You said it…'

And Sophie knew beyond a doubt that he'd thought it. He hadn't been able to disguise the surprise in his eyes when she'd shown she really did know how to perform CPR.

'My father's a doctor. He taught us all what to do in emergency situations. I've never had to do it for real…' She couldn't keep the trace of bitterness from her tone. Her father had always assumed she'd become a doctor, and instead she'd taken up a profession that had no value in his eyes. His only response to the news that she was making this film had been a back-handed compliment, saying he was glad she was at least pretending to do something useful.

'Well remembered, then.'

He smiled, and pleasure trickled across the dull pain of rejection. Sophie wondered whether he'd adjust his opinion if he knew that she was still searching her mind for his first name. Dr Taylor seemed a little formal, since they'd just saved the life of a props dummy together.

'As you already have a good idea of how to resuscitate someone, you understand the theory behind it all.'

'Yes.' Sophie nodded. When he put it that way, she supposed that she did.

'Which will stand you in really good stead for this.' He got to his feet, producing a copy of the medical techniques document. She'd studied her copy for hours, hoping that she might retain at least some of it. 'I guess you haven't had much of a chance to look at it.'

'No. Not really.' He was giving her a way out, and Sophie took it gratefully.

He grinned. 'I guess that's my job. It gives a detailed description of how resuscitation was carried out in the nineteen-forties—which is a little different from the way we do it now.'

'They did chest compressions but no rescue breaths.' A fragment of fact suddenly popped into her mind.

He nodded. 'Yes, I've managed to find a couple of old training films on the internet. But it may be easier to just try it ourselves.' He knelt down next to her. 'Do you want to start with the compressions?'

'Okay.' Sophie could do that. She already knew how to do compressions. This morning was going a lot better than she'd expected it to. No tantrums needed to cover her lapses in memory, and the doctor seemed to be going out of his way not to spring anything unexpected on her.

'Right, then.' He flashed her a grin. 'Here we go...'

The morning's work had been a success. Starting with what Sophie knew and then using gesture and movement to reinforce the new information seemed to have worked. The atmosphere on set lightened considerably as she sailed through her scene that afternoon, even managing to bestow a few smiles on her co-star and the crew.

Joel, the director, spared a nod of satisfaction for Drew, clearly pleased with his tutelage. Carly gave him a beaming smile when she thought no one else was looking, and Sophie ignored him completely.

Even though she clearly didn't want to think about him unless she absolutely had to, Sophie dominated Drew's thoughts. He watched her carefully, and as dispassionately as he could. And the more he watched her, the more he realised that he knew what was wrong, and that she was trying desperately to cover it up.

CHAPTER FOUR

THE FOLLOWING DAY didn't start well. The script had said rain, but real rain seemed to be a problem, and an unscheduled downpour had stopped filming for a while. Rumour had it that Carly was confined to her room at the hotel with a stomach bug, and Sophie's face was set in a hard, concentrated frown. She avoided him as if he had something catching.

Joel had called cut, and the clapperboard signalled the tenth rerun of a scene that should have been easy. Each time she'd fluffed her lines Sophie's air of prickly uninterest had increased markedly.

'It's all a matter of…' She stopped suddenly, frowning. 'This isn't right, Joel.'

'Oh, for goodness' sake…' Todd Hunter, her co-star, turned away suddenly, frustration and anger showing on his face. Joel moved in to smooth things over.

'What's the matter, Sophie?'

'It's not right… Give me the script…' Sophie looked as if she was about to burst into tears.

A copy of the script appeared out of nowhere, and Sophie leafed through it, seemingly too dissatisfied to find the right page, and then threw it to one side. Drew got to his feet, navigating through the circle of cameras and sound technicians around her.

'It's nearly lunchtime. We'll take a break.' Joel seemed resigned to handling Sophie's moods and perhaps he thought that the catering truck could do what he couldn't and get today on a better footing. 'Sophie…'

Joel's mouth quirked in an expression of helplessness as he found himself speaking to thin air. Sophie was already on her way to her trailer, cutting a swathe into the crowd around her as they moved to get out of her way.

Jennie, a bright, usually happy young woman, who had introduced herself yesterday to Drew as Sophie's assistant, ran after her. He saw Sophie turn, aiming a couple of angry words in Jennie's direction and gesturing to her to go away. Jennie fell back, her face reddening, and Drew frowned. That kind of behaviour really wasn't necessary.

Drew pushed through the groups of people who were putting some distance between themselves and Sophie. She could act up with Joel, and he'd try to smooth things over to get her co-operation. Everyone else would cave in to her tantrums, in fear for their jobs. But this was one job he didn't need to keep.

Dammit! One curse vied with another in her head, filling her thoughts with the kind of obscenities that she never spoke out loud. She was turning into a monster. Slowly and irrevocably, and there was nothing she could do to stop it.

'Sophie…'

The one voice she didn't want to hear. The doctor. Damn him, too.

'Sophie…?'

He didn't give up, did he? She was twenty feet from her trailer and then she could slam the door in his face, lock him out.

She didn't make it. With just a couple of paces to go before she reached safety, she felt his hand on her arm.

'Let go of me.' She whipped her arm away as if he'd grabbed it, not just touched it lightly.

'Wait, Sophie.'

His tone was so sure, so commanding, and in a sea of misunderstandings and unknowns it was the only thing that seemed to make any sense. Despite herself, she stopped.

'You haven't figured out how things work around here yet, have you?' She glared at him. 'I'm at the top of the pecking order and you're at the bottom. You don't tell me what to do.'

That bloody smile again. Relaxed and assured, the smile of a man who already knew his place in the world and didn't need anyone to tell him what it was. And dangerous in the extreme. 'I thought that was exactly my role. I'm an advisor and so I advise.'

'Don't be smart with me.' Sophie rolled her eyes and turned away from him, as if what he'd just said didn't deserve a proper answer. That always seemed to work when she couldn't come up with the words she wanted.

He slipped past her, opening the door of her trailer and walking inside. *Her private trailer.* The only place where she could take some refuge from the noise and bustle of the set. Panic started to rise in her chest.

'Get. Out.'

'There seems to be something wrong. I'd like to help.'

'I don't need help.' Anger wasn't working, and she tried another tack. Right on cue she summoned tears and a look of melting supplication. 'Please, go…'

He smiled, sitting down in one of the comfortable armchairs in the seating area. 'Nice one. You're very good.'

'What's that supposed to mean?' Sophie scowled at him.

'It means that you're a tremendous actress. And that you'll do anything to stop anyone finding out the difficulties you're having right now. Only I see through it.'

If he'd had any doubts about his conclusions before, the mock tears and that look of seductive pleading banished them altogether. She knew exactly what was wrong with her. If he could get through to her, just talk to her and make her see sense, then he'd be out of here in a week and back to a world where sanity was more of a guiding principle.

She sat down opposite him. That was something. Sitting was better than running.

'Who sent you to spy on me? Who are you reporting to?'

'No one. It's not like that at all, Sophie. When Carly spoke to me she mentioned…'

Wrong move. All the colour drained from Sophie's face and her hand flew to her mouth. Tears formed in her eyes and this time they looked like the real thing.

'Carly…? No…'

'Carly happened to mention that you were under a bit of stress.' That was stretching the truth to breaking point, but he'd already landed Carly in enough hot water.

Sophie stared at him blankly. Drew had seen that look before, when everything became too much and someone started to shut down.

'Sophie, listen to me. It's okay…'

'You think that any of this is okay?' she flashed back at him.

Time for the truth. 'All right. I don't know anything for sure, but here's what I think I know. You're having difficulties with your short-term memory. The things you've known for a while are no problem, it's new information that you can't process properly. It's possible that you sustained a mild traumatic brain injury in your recent car accident.'

'Carly just happened to mention that as well?' She'd composed herself now, and was staring straight at him.

'She's a good friend to you, Sophie, and she's trying to help you.' If he could do nothing else, at least he could try to repair the damage he'd done. So far he'd only managed to isolate Sophie even further from the one person who seemed to care about her.

'Whatever. That's not really your business, is it?'

'No, it's just an observation.'

'Yes, it's all just observations, isn't it? I think it's all in your imagination.'

'What's my name, Sophie?'

She shot him a defiant look. 'Dr…'

'My name.'

'What do I care?' She looked as if she was about to launch into another diatribe about how *she* was the important person around here, and his status was that of a cockroach, when a knock sounded on the door.

'Catering…'

'Come in.' Sophie pulled herself together and gave the young woman who entered a composed smile, watching as she set a covered plate on the table and got water from the fridge in the tiny kitchenette at the far end of the living space.

'Would you bring another plate, please?'

'For Dr Taylor? Sure.' The woman turned to Drew. 'What would you like?'

'Anything's fine.' Sophie's sudden turnaround was a surprise, but if accepting lunch meant that she was going to let him stay a while longer then he would eat whatever anyone put in front of him.

'Chicken in a cream sauce, sautéed potatoes, green beans…?'

'Sounds great. Thank you.'

The woman nodded. 'Back in a tick.'

He picked up the bottle of water from the table and filled her glass, aware that she was watching every move he made. 'Thank you.'

'Don't get any ideas. It's only lunch. We're not best friends yet.'

'I know.' She'd obviously come to the conclusion that she couldn't get rid of him so she was calling a truce. Drew nodded at her plate. 'Don't wait for me, yours will get cold.'

* * *

He knew. It was one thing for people to speculate, but he was a doctor and his word held some weight. And he wasn't just speculating, he knew. The only way out of this mess was to stop denying the obvious and try to get him to keep quiet about it.

Lunch gave her an opportunity to think. The doctor never mentioned anything to do with her memory until they were sipping their coffee, but Sophie knew this was temporary. He was biding his time, in just the same way she was.

'There's something I have to know.'

'Okay.' He handed her the mint chocolate that had come with his coffee. He must have noticed that she'd eaten hers straight away. He seemed to notice far too much.

'I need you to be discreet.' She unwrapped the chocolate, nibbling at the edge of it.

He nodded. 'Carly's already taken care of that.' He reached into his pocket, taking out a couple of sheets of paper, stapled together. Sophie wondered if he'd been carrying them around with him in anticipation of just this moment.

She scanned them carefully. A standard confidentiality agreement, with his signature and Carly's on the bottom. 'You plan to honour this?'

'Yes. Even without it, anything you say is confidential. I'm a doctor.'

'I don't recall asking for your professional services.' The jibe came out of nowhere, from the place where everything was a threat and no one could be trusted.

'No, you didn't. I'm offering them anyway.'

She shrugged. 'Do you understand how dangerous rumours like this can be? No one wants to employ an actress who can't remember what comes next. In big-budget projects like this, it's too much of a financial risk.'

'I understand. And it doesn't matter what your reasons are. Confidentiality is confidentiality.'

Sophie supposed that she would have to take him at his word. 'I want to make it clear that I've never taken drugs and I don't have an alcohol problem. My accident was nothing to do with either of those things.'

'Okay.'

'You believe me?'

'Yes.'

'Right. Thanks.' He could have believed her in a few more words but a yes would do. It was unequivocal enough, particularly when said the way he'd said it.

'I know it's tough, Sophie. When you remember some things and not others in what seems to be a completely random way. And the toughest thing is knowing that your memory's not working properly, and never being sure if there's something you've missed.'

'If you say so.' Actually, that was a pretty good description of how she felt. Never being sure of anything.

'Is it all right if I ask you some questions?'

'If I say no, you'll only ask them anyway. So you'd better get on with it.'

'Okay.' He grinned at her, and suddenly it seemed so much easier to just go along with him. He did have a very nice smile. 'This all started around the time of your accident?'

'Yes. It was much worse at first, and it's been improving over time.' There had been no recurrence of the lost days that she'd experienced right after the accident. And she didn't want to tell him about them. She didn't even want to think about the photographs that had appeared on the internet afterwards. Sophie couldn't bear to see the judgement in his beautiful grey eyes.

'Any clumsiness, loss of co-ordination?'

'I used to drop things quite a lot. And I'd forget how to

do little things, like how to turn the shower on. I knew about traumatic brain injury from my father talking about it, and I knew that I could practise and relearn things.'

'That must have been very hard to do on your own.'

'I'm an actress, I've been taught how to be aware of movement and gesture.'

'Even so, it's a huge achievement. You should be proud of yourself.'

'Thanks.' This was the first time that someone had understood. The first time that anyone had praised her for the little things that had been so hard for her. She felt lighter than she had done for a very long time.

'That's good to see too…'

'What?'

'Your smile.' His gaze dropped from her face, as if that was the one thing he was embarrassed to have noticed. 'You've never seen a doctor about any of this?'

'No. I have to keep it quiet.'

'I understand that but you need to have a proper diagnosis. I can arrange for you to see someone discreetly. No one will know.'

'I'll think about it.'

'Don't put this off, Sophie.'

'I'll think about it. Don't push me. I can still have you thrown off the set.'

His gaze held hers for a moment, and then let go. They both knew she wouldn't do that now.

'All right. So shall we concentrate on getting through today, then? Leave the other things until later.'

That would be good. 'What do you suggest?'

'Why don't you lie down for half an hour then I'll go through your lines with you. See if we can crack this scene together.'

The way he'd helped her with the CPR scene. She did

need some help, and he seemed to know how to fix memories into her head.

'Okay. Thank you.'

Drew found Joel eating a sandwich and talking to one of the cameramen. With the practised instincts of a man who missed nothing of what was going on around the set, Joel propped his plate on top of his script and rose to meet him.

'How's Sophie?'

'Fine. She's calmed down and I suggested she take a rest for a while. She'll be ready to start work in an hour.'

'You're sure about that? If she's going to be spending the whole afternoon in her trailer, I'd rather know now.' Joel eyed him suspiciously.

'I'm sure. She'll be back here in an hour.'

'Okay, thanks. Keep me informed, will you?'

'Of course.' Drew turned before Joel could ask any other awkward questions. The next task, was make sure that Sophie was word perfect and ready to face the world in exactly one hour.

CHAPTER FIVE

THE HAMMERING ON the door of his hotel room was insistent. Drew looked at the travelling clock at his bedside. Half past eleven. Probably someone who'd just been ejected from the hotel bar.

'Please… It's Sophie…' When he hadn't answered immediately, the knocking got louder, and Sophie's voice sounded through the door, propelling him out of bed and onto his feet.

'What…?' He stepped back as she almost fell into the room. If she'd decided that seducing him would get him to let up on her, a white cotton nightie with a long cardigan over the top of it wasn't the obvious choice of outfit, but on Sophie it looked entrancing. Something at the back of his mind screamed that being alone in a hotel room, half-naked, with a scantily dressed film star who had a patchy memory showed spectacularly bad judgement.

'It's Carly. She's sick. Please, come.' She frowned at him. 'Put some clothes on.'

He was beginning to like it when Sophie put him firmly in his place. Drew reached for his jeans, dragging them on over his boxer shorts, and caught up a T-shirt. 'What's the matter?'

'I don't know. She seemed better this evening. Her room's next to my suite and I left the adjoining door open and went to bed. When I woke up just now I heard her crying. She's in such pain…'

'Okay, which way?' Drew hoped she could remember, because he had no idea where Carly's room was.

She led the way through a maze of corridors, taking a few wrong turns before she reached one of the rooms at the front of the hotel. Carly was curled up on the bed, her knees almost touching her chin, tears streaking her cheeks. Untypically for someone who was obviously feeling very ill, she didn't look particularly pleased to see a doctor.

'I'm all right. It's just a…' Whatever Carly thought she might be suffering from was lost as she caught her breath in pain.

'Okay, then. Let's just have a look.'

Carly resisted him, and Sophie's voice sounded, firm and calm. 'Stop messing about and just do what the doctor tells you.'

'You're a fine one to talk.' Carly cursed under her breath but she let Drew roll her over on the bed and pull her hand from her side.

'Is this where it hurts?'

'Yeah…'

He pressed gently and Carly winced. When he removed the pressure she cried out in pain. Drew didn't need a thermometer to tell him that she was running a fever, burning up.

'Sophie, do you have your phone?'

'I think so.' She looked in the pocket of her cardigan and found it, handing it over to Drew. He dialled quickly, telling the ambulance controller that he was a doctor and that he had a patient with all the signs of acute appendicitis.

'Get off…my case…' Carly paused to catch her breath. 'It's a stomach bug. I'll be fine in the morning. I'm not going anywhere.'

'Carly, you're sick. Please.' Sophie was standing behind him, close to tears now. 'You have to go.'

'Soph…' Carly was clearly in a lot of pain, but all she could think about was her friend.

'Look, Carly. I know you brought him here to help me, and I've told him everything.'

'You told...*him*?'

'Wasn't that your plan all along?' Drew wondered whether he should leave the room to allow the two of them to argue about him in private.

'None of that matters now, Carly. Since the accident, I can't remember stuff, but I've admitted it now, and everything's going to be okay. You have to go. Please, I promise I'll let the doctor help me.' The words tumbled from Sophie's mouth in a rush of anxiety for her friend.

'Is that true?' Carly looked at Drew.

'It's true. You need to go with the ambulance. I'll look after Sophie.'

'You only signed for a week...'

'Forget the contract. I'm staying here until you're well.'

Carly gave a small nod and let him roll her over onto her side, drawing her knees up in a position that would make the pain easier for her to bear. Sophie pushed past him, getting onto the bed and holding her friend as best she could.

'Hang onto me, honey. It's going to be all right.'

Tears began to roll down Carly's cheeks, and she started to sob. 'I want Mark...'

'I know you do. We'll call him as soon as we have you safe in the hospital.' She turned her head towards Drew. 'Mark DeAngelo, Carly's husband. His number's in my phone. Will you remember that I have to call him?'

'I'll remember.'

It had taken this for Sophie and Carly to finally talk to each other. Drew watched the two of them, curled up together on the bed, holding each other tightly, and hoped that Sophie would remember at least something about her promise to take some help.

The ambulance crew arrived and Sophie slipped away, letting Drew talk to the woman paramedic. He could hear her banging around in the suite next door and he resolved that he'd go and see what she was up to as soon as he could.

'Okay.' The paramedic bent over Carly. 'Carly…Carly, we're going to take you to hospital. The stretcher's coming up now and we'll get you comfortable and carry you down to the ambulance.'

Carly nodded wordlessly. She was lying quietly now, which wasn't necessarily a good sign. Sudden relief of pain usually occurred when the appendix burst, and Drew wouldn't put it past her to give a busy A and E department the slip and simply walk out of there.

A noise behind him made him glance around. Sophie was standing in the doorway, fully dressed, her designer handbag slung across her body, looking as if she was planning on going somewhere. That was all he needed. Drew had no intention of letting Carly go to the hospital alone, but Sophie was only going to get in the way.

'Sophie…' He walked towards her, leaving the paramedic to tend to Carly. 'I want you to stay here.'

'Forget it.'

'The ambulance won't take two passengers.'

'Then I'll get a taxi and follow you.'

Like hell she would. Having Sophie wandering around a strange hospital in the middle of the night wasn't his idea of looking after her.

'I can't watch out for both of you at the same time. Work with me, Sophie. I want to go with Carly to make sure she's all right, but I can't do that if I'm not confident that you're going to stay here.'

Her defiant, odd-eyed gaze met his. 'Okay, then.' She pushed past him, waiting for the paramedic to finish with Carly.

'Would you mind if I came in the ambulance too. Please? She's my friend. And he's a doctor, so he doesn't really count as a passenger.'

The paramedic flipped her gaze towards Drew, who nodded grudgingly, and then grinned at Sophie. 'Okay. I can make an exception this once.'

The A and E doctor's reaction was just as Drew had expected. He examined Carly and then got straight onto the phone. Sophie had hung onto Carly's hand, comforting her, and even though Carly had protested that they should go, she was clearly relieved that neither of them would.

He'd noticed that Sophie had kept her head down and walked close to him as they'd hurried through the busy public area of the hospital, and also that the nurse who attended Carly obviously recognised her. Nothing had been said, though, and he was grateful that Sophie had been allowed the space to be just another worried friend.

That anonymity was ripped away from her as soon as Carly was taken away for an emergency appendectomy, and Sophie walked back through into the waiting room. A girl, who looked too young for the short skirt and sequinned top that she was wearing, came straight up to her, grabbing her arm.

'You're Sophie Warner…' Her face was flushed and her eyes shone.

If Sophie was surprised, she didn't show it. Somehow she managed to extricate herself from the girl's grip without making a big thing of it and smiled as if she'd just met a long-lost friend.

'My friends said I shouldn't speak to you.' The girl gestured towards a group of half a dozen teenagers sitting in the corner of the waiting room, all dressed up to the nines and all staring at Sophie. 'But I still love you…'

In spite of what the papers said. In spite of what her friends said. Sophie's resigned half-shrug indicated that she had a pretty good idea of how the conversation between the girls must have gone.

'I'm so glad you did come over to say hello. What's your name?'

'Gillian.'

'Gillian.' Sophie shot Drew a glance as she repeated the name, and he made a mental note, in case he needed to prompt her with it later. 'Thank you for believing in me.'

The blush spread from Gillian's cheeks to the roots of her hair. 'I said it wasn't true.'

'All my real friends know that it isn't.'

Sophie had barely got the words out before Gillian flung her arms around her, enveloping her in a hug. Drew stepped forward to intervene and then saw Sophie's face. Eyes squeezed shut, to hide her tears.

Gillian let go of her and produced a phone from her pocket. 'Can I have a photo?'

The girls in the corner were talking excitedly now, and one of them was already weaving unsteadily on her high heels past the rows of seats. The situation was about to turn into a commotion.

'Let's go over there.' Sophie indicated an empty alcove, which contained a drinks machine and some chairs. 'We don't want to cause a disturbance.'

She seemed to have won the girls over completely. Sophie walked quickly over to the alcove, sitting down in the corner, and they followed her like a swarm of heat-seeking missiles. Drew kept as close as he could to Sophie, but he was elbowed out of the way, and she was surrounded.

It was impossible to say which one of them needed the services of the A and E department. They were chattering excitedly and Sophie quieted them, making a good-humoured game out of not drawing attention to themselves.

She smiled, hugging Gillian, while the girl took selfies. Then went to sit down next to one of other girls. Drew saw that her tights were ripped and she had blood caked on her leg.

'You fell over?' Sophie had disregarded the large graze on her knee and was looking at an inch-long cut on her cheekbone. 'Have you seen a doctor yet?'

'Yes.' The girl wriggled with pleasure at her concern. 'I've got to wait to have it stitched. It takes so long, though. I want to go home.'

'No, you must stay here,' Sophie reproved her gently.

'Do you think so?' Sophie's opinion was obviously more important to the girl than anything the doctors could possibly say to her.

'Yes, I do. Would you like a photo?'

The girl proffered her phone uncertainly, her hand wandering to the cut on her face, and Sophie handed the phone to Drew. 'Would you do it?'

He bent down to take the shot. Sophie put her arm around the girl, and they put their heads together, cheek to cheek. Then she waved Drew to the right a little, and he realised that at this angle the cut wouldn't show at all.

He took three shots, just in case, and handed the phone back. Sophie took it, expressed delight with two of the images and disappointment with the third, gently suggesting that it might be deleted.

'Those two are great. Thank you…' The girl flung her arms around Sophie and kissed her cheek, and phones were raised to capture the moment.

'Are you someone?' Drew found that he was suddenly the object of everyone's attention.

'He's a doctor.' Sophie leaned in, as if she was imparting an important secret.

'Is he your boyfriend?'

Drew felt the back of his neck start to itch with embarrassment. A simple enough question, with a simple enough answer. Why did it make him feel so uncomfortable?

'No, he's here with my friend. She was taken ill tonight.'

'Is she all right?'

Finally. Someone had thought that Sophie might have more important things to think about than taking selfies and signing autographs.

'Yes, she's going to be fine. But I have to go and check on what's happening with her now.'

The girls were unwilling to let her go, and it was time for Drew to step in. Allowing each of them one final hug, and the girl who had cut her face a few words of comfort and reassurance from Sophie, he put his arm around her shoulder and guided her away.

She looked suddenly tired. He felt her body trembling with fatigue against his, and he wrapped his jacket around her shoulders, hoping that they could get out of there before anyone else recognised her.

'Are we waiting?' She pulled his jacket around her.

'No, Carly's in surgery. And she'll be sleeping for some time after that. We can come back in the morning.' He adopted a firm tone. There was no more they could do here and Sophie had already had enough for tonight.

'Yes. I feel… I'm sorry. I feel so tired.'

'We're going back to the hotel, right now.' Drew guided her through the doors and towards a taxi rank, where one solitary taxi waited, its driver lounging against the side of the car. He hurried her across, thankfully managing to get the driver's attention before anyone else got there, and put her into the back of the cab.

Sophie opened her eyes and then closed them again. Hotel room. Yeah, she knew where she was. Slowly she oriented herself, not searching for the memories, just letting them come in their own sweet time.

'Carly!' She sat up in bed, pulling the bedspread off herself, and realised that she was still fully clothed, apart from her shoes, which lay neatly on the floor beside the bed.

She covered her face with her hands. She remembered now. She'd fallen asleep in the taxi, and woken to find him carrying her upstairs. She'd snuggled into his arms, letting him lay her on the bed and take off her shoes.

'Hey…' Sophie froze. That was his voice. He was still

there. 'It's okay, everything's fine. We took Carly to hospital last night with appendicitis and she had an emergency operation.'

Yes, she remembered that. She still wasn't sure what had happened after he'd taken her shoes off, though. The thought of another night that she couldn't remember made her feel sick.

'You're…' Still here? Dressed? He was clearly both, but Sophie was lost for a way to enquire tactfully as to whether the latter had changed at some point during the night.

She still had her jeans on. And she could feel her bra strap under her T-shirt. No one had sex and then put their clothes back on to go to sleep…

'You went to sleep in the taxi. I brought you up here and stayed around to fill you in on the details when you woke up.' He was sitting in the large armchair tucked in the corner of the room, and Sophie noticed that one of the pillows from the bed was propped under his shoulders.

'That's it?' Perhaps she was panicking over nothing. There was nothing to indicate that she'd forgotten anything, only the uncomfortable knowledge that she was quite capable of doing so.

'Yes. That's it. You opened your eyes when I took your shoes off, and then you went right back to sleep.'

So there really was nothing to remember. Relief was tainted by guilt. 'I should have stayed awake. At least until Carly was out of surgery.'

'You were exhausted.'

'I haven't been sleeping all that well recently.' Sophie pressed her lips together, aware that she'd probably just admitted to another of the symptoms of traumatic brain injury. She should be a bit more careful.

'I need to phone the hospital and see how Carly is.' She looked around for her bag and spotted it beside the bed.

'I've done that already. She's fine. She came through the operation with flying colours and she's sleeping now. And the last thing you did before you went to sleep in the taxi was to give me your phone and ask me to call Carly's husband.'

'Mark's okay?'

'Yes. He's worried, of course, but I texted him this morning to let him know how she was and give him the number for the hospital.'

'Thanks. I'll call him later. When can I go and see Carly? She'll want to speak to him.'

'You can go and see her whenever you want. We've got the day off today.'

That she'd forgotten. Her eyes wandered to the clock on the nightstand. As it was nine o'clock and no one had come to hammer on her door yet, she supposed he must be right. She twisted the corners of her mouth downwards.

'I forgot. Sorry...'

He shrugged, as if it didn't matter. 'I can't think you're the only one who woke up this morning thinking there was somewhere else they ought to be.'

She doubted she was. But for most people the information came to them. She had absolutely no idea what day it was, and, however hard she tried, she couldn't work it out.

'It's Saturday.' He walked towards the bed and sat down on it, holding her phone out towards her. Sophie took it quickly, trying not to either visibly shrink from him or get too close.

'Thanks. Saturday.'

'What do you say we meet downstairs for breakfast in half an hour? Then I'll take you to see Carly.'

'Breakfast would be nice. But I can get a taxi to the hospital.'

'I'll take you.' He smiled, and suddenly she felt very alone with him. 'I'm not having Carly discharging herself over some mistaken idea that she's needed here.'

'I can manage.'

'We've been through this one already. I told Carly I'd look after you.'

'I appreciate that, but it was only to get her to go. I'm not going to hold you to it.'

'You promised you'd let me look after you. I'm going to hold you to that.' His gaze slid towards her handbag. 'You want to write that down?'

He'd noticed the notebook, then. Of course he had.

'No, I'll remember.' Sophie scrambled off the bed and he took the hint, following her into the sitting-room.

'Half an hour. Breakfast. If you don't turn up, I'll come and get you.' He grinned at her, and disappeared through the door of her suite.

CHAPTER SIX

HOWEVER MUCH HE tried to keep it simple, things seemed to be getting more complicated by the minute. Initially, Drew had made up his mind he disliked Sophie and that she was a beautiful, spoilt star, who needed a good shake. Then grudging respect had begun to creep in. Sophie might be volatile and difficult, but she was facing impossible obstacles, and it had taken a lot of guts for her to get this far.

Now he found himself wishing that Carly could be persuaded to go away and recuperate for a couple of weeks, so he could get to know Sophie a bit better. It was the start of a very steep and slippery slope, and what made it even more hazardous was that he had no intention of changing his course now.

He took the day slow and easy. A late breakfast and then a taxi ride to the hospital to see Carly. Sophie went to her room to rest in the afternoon, and met him downstairs for dinner.

Drew selected their table carefully, in a quiet corner of the hotel patio. They could talk there, without being overheard, and, more importantly, the area was a little removed from the noise and bustle of the main restaurant. Sophie would be able to gather her thoughts better there.

Joel joined them for dessert, chatting about nothing but watching Sophie carefully. When he rose, after fifteen minutes, to move on to another table, he gave Drew an almost imperceptible nod, which Drew studiedly ignored.

'He's doing the rounds.' Sophie leaned towards Drew slightly, speaking quietly. 'Have you noticed that he generally sits down with everyone at least once a day? Doesn't say much of any importance but he listens a lot.'

'Yes, I'd noticed.' Drew grinned at her. 'MBWA.'

'What's that?'

'Management By Walking Around. If you do it right, you get to know a lot about what's going on.'

She was watching Joel thoughtfully as he meandered across the dining room, her expression taking on an almost haunted quality. 'I have to be so careful.'

'About what?'

'That I don't give any clues…' She was twisting her fingers together in her lap. 'If Joel works it out…'

'You haven't worked it out properly yet. You're assuming that you have a brain injury.' Drew didn't really want to go into the other things that might cause a loss of short-term memory. It was unlikely, particularly in the context that Sophie's condition was improving. But they had to be ruled out.

'That's what makes sense. My father—'

'I know. Your father told you all about brain injuries. Have you considered that he might also tell you that self-diagnosing is never a good idea?'

'He doesn't think anything that I do is a good idea. I'm used to that.' Sophie's face took on a pinched look. 'I still think I should read up a bit so I know what I'm pretending not to have.'

Reading up on the many and varied symptoms of traumatic brain injury, and concentrating on not showing any of them, really wasn't the way to go. It would just put Sophie under even more stress. 'I think that's a bit paranoid, isn't it?'

The last vestiges of the easy atmosphere that had kept them going throughout the day dissolved into the night air. 'You think I'm paranoid?'

'No, I didn't mean that…'

'You said it.' Her face was blank of emotion. Drew had

come to see that as a warning sign. 'Perhaps paranoia is just another symptom, eh? Or maybe it's just a hazard of my job.'

Before Drew could find a way to disagree convincingly, she stood up. Avoiding his gaze, Sophie marched away through the dining room and out into the hotel lobby.

Drew had spent the last hour shut away in his room, deep in thought. Each time he considered it anew, the conundrum seemed to unravel a little, then twist itself into an even more torturous set of questions.

He wasn't maintaining a proper professional distance. He was reacting like someone who was emotionally involved.

He *was* emotionally involved. He couldn't help it. She'd walked away from him, and he was angry with her like some spurned suitor, instead of understanding the issues the way a doctor should.

He jumped as a knock sounded through the door. 'Room Service. Room 339.'

The voice calling was heavily accented and Drew shook his head. Wrong room. Someone else was waiting for whatever the woman outside had brought him.

He went to the door and opened it. Sophie was there, wearing a pair of stunningly high black court shoes, which brought the top of her head up to the level of his cheekbone. Neat black slacks and a white shirt with a scarf tied at the neck, in the manner of the waitresses in the hotel. A napkin over one arm, and a large tray in her hands.

'You missed out on coffee after dinner.' Something in her eyes begged him not to slam the door in her face, however much he was tempted to. And Drew couldn't resist Sophie's eyes.

'Yes, I did.' He stood back from the doorway, and she walked past him into the room, setting the tray down on the small table by the window, next to the chair he'd been sitting in.

She poured the coffee and turned to him. 'Milk and sugar, sir?'

If she was going to play the waitress, she may as well get it right. Most of the staff here knew his name, and used it. It was only Sophie who didn't seem to be able to get her head around it, and that felt like a personal slight.

'No one else around here calls me sir…' The words slipped out before he could stop them.

A flicker at the side of her eye betrayed that she knew he was angry. 'No. Of course… Milk and sugar… Taylor?'

It was as if she'd jabbed a pin into his over-inflated pride. He'd belittled her, asking for something that everyone else found so simple and she found horribly difficult. And instead of running away, she'd done the best she could. It was an odd mixture of defiance and a heart-wrenching attempt to please.

'I'll take it black thanks, Warner. Will you join me?'

She nodded, splashing coffee into the other cup on the tray and perching herself on the edge of the second chair by the table. Her coffee cup rattled a little in the saucer as she picked it up and Drew realised that she was shaking.

'I'm sorry, Sophie.'

'No… You're right…'

'Drew.' He helped her this time, smiling as he did so.

'Yes. Drew.' A single crease of concentration appeared on her brow. 'I knew it was something like that. I don't know why I keep forgetting it.'

'It doesn't matter, Sophie. You can call me any damn thing you like, I know that it's not your fault.'

She nodded. 'I want to get it right, though. Drew.'

'Short for Andrew. Only my parents only ever called me Drew, and it stuck.'

'I prefer Drew.'

'So do I.' Now that the layers of defiance and fear had been peeled away, she seemed very sad. Very hurt. Drew's heart ached for hers.

'It's all a matter of finding hooks to hang the memories

onto. They can be jokes, or visual images, or gestures. Whatever works for you.'

She thought for a moment. 'It's that easy?'

'No, it's not easy. But you can do it.'

She took another sip of her coffee, her brow creased in thought. He wanted to kiss away the stress, replace it with quite a different kind of tension, but those thoughts were unacceptable. Instead, he picked up his coffee cup.

She hadn't messed everything up after all. Sophie had stormed to her room, found her notebook and scribbled crossly in it so she wouldn't forget how angry she was with him. Then she'd scored the words out. He was probably right.

Anyone in her position *would* be paranoid. Photographs of her naked, on the internet, that she couldn't remember being taken, the press hounding her, everyone believing the lies. But when she was with him, it was as if all that didn't exist.

She drank her coffee, allowing the good feelings to seep in, displacing the bad. She hadn't said what she'd come to say to him yet.

'I'm sorry...Drew.'

He grinned. However much he said he didn't care what she called him, he clearly did.

'I know I shouldn't just walk away when things get difficult. It's rude and dismissive.' She took a deep breath. 'I know I don't have any second chances left, but if I asked you for just one more...'

'You've got it. And you didn't have to ask.'

'Thank you. I appreciate that.'

He reached towards her, tipping her chin up gently. His gaze was right there, with all the warmth she hadn't dared hope to see.

'I'll be there for you, Sophie.'

'You'll help me? If I promise to try and do better, you'll hold me to that?'

He chuckled. 'I'll hold you to it.'

'Thank you.' Relief couldn't stop the mist of fatigue that was descending on her, and the coffee wasn't helping either. 'I feel really tired. I…think I probably ought to go now.'

He put his cup down, grinning. 'I'll walk you to your suite. Do you need a wake-up call in the morning?'

'Carly usually…' Carly wasn't here. 'I can get the hotel to send someone up.' Hopefully whoever it was wouldn't leave until she was on her feet and talking coherently. Just having her eyes open was no guarantee that she wouldn't doze off again for another couple of hours, however hard she tried not to.

'No need. Wake-up calls are my speciality.' Something about the sudden glint in his eye told Sophie that they probably were.

Sophie was grateful that he didn't keep her talking at the door of her suite. When she tried to stifle a yawn he smiled and pocketed the key she'd given him, his parting goodnight aimed over his shoulder. When she bade him goodnight in return he raised one hand in a signal that he'd heard, without looking back.

Turn, turn, turn…

Drew wasn't going to. The swing doors at the end of the corridor would have been an ideal place to look back, but he missed the cue. Took those comfortably wide shoulders and his slim hips through the doors and out of sight. Sophie sighed. Her co-star, Todd Hunter, would have milked the moment and turned to flash his trademark smile, but suddenly that seemed like overkill. Drew was a better hero any day of the week.

She might have to revise that assessment. Sophie had slept for three hours then spent another three tossing and turning in her bed. It seemed that she'd only just closed her eyes, when she felt a hand on her shoulder, gently shaking her.

'No…'

'Coffee.' His voice was firm. She could smell the coffee. Sophie squeezed her eyes shut.

'I can't. Leave me alone.'

'Yes, you can. If you wake up at the proper time, it'll help you to sleep at the proper time.'

'Go away. It's too early for advice.'

She felt his arm around her shoulders. He smelled of soap. Gorgeous. Before Sophie could wriggle free of him, she was sitting up in bed. He was a lot more gentle about this than Carly generally was.

'Come on. Open your eyes.'

She opened one, and saw his smile. Maybe that was worth opening the other for. He proffered the cup, and she took a sip of coffee.

Then he was gone. The sound of the shower running in the bathroom reached her ears. No way…

By the time he got back she had disentangled one foot from the duvet, and it was hanging over the edge of the bed. She felt his fingers brush her instep and heard him chuckle. Then he lifted her out of the bed, setting her onto her feet.

'Okay? Can I let go of you?'

Actually, she'd prefer it if he didn't, his arms were so warm. But she was steady enough on her feet. 'Yeah. I'm fine.'

'Okay. Coffee.' He handed her the cup and she took another sip. 'Now walk a bit.'

She was wide awake now. 'All right. I've got it. I can take it from here.'

'I'll see you downstairs for breakfast.' He turned on his heel, and was gone, closing the door quietly behind him.

He must have been studying the script. Drew was not only word perfect with her part, but with everyone else's. At lunchtime, they sat together in her trailer, his smile rewarding her when she got things right and carrying her over the bits where she stumbled.

'Almost…' He didn't even seem to notice that this was

the third time she'd fluffed that particular line. 'Imagine Todd in a tank of water. With piranhas nibbling at his toes. *I can't help you with that…*'

Sophie snorted with laughter. 'Okay…*I can't help you with that. You have to find your own way...*'

'*And do it…?*'

'*And do it quickly.*' She grinned at Drew. 'The piranhas will be up to your knees if you don't.'

'Okay, what's next?' He covered her copy of the script with his hand.

'Long spiel from Todd… He's torn between…'

'The piranhas and the shark that's circling, over there.' He jerked his thumb behind him.

'Oh. Big tank of water, then?'

'Yep, big as you like. Now what?'

'*I can't save you, Todd.*' The image of her own character in a lifejacket floated into her head and she hung onto that.

'Great. Perfect. Shall we try it again, from the top?'

She'd thought this scene was going to be a killer. But with the help of the images that Drew put into her head, the movements that he associated with the lines, the whole thing seemed, quite literally, to take shape. He was liberal with his praise and patient when she stumbled. When it was time to do the scene for real, in front of the cameras, she sailed through it.

'You did brilliantly.' He was sitting in a fold-up chair on the edge of the set and Sophie sat down next to him.

'Thanks. The piranhas helped.'

That grin of his, which seemed to frame the day, keep her on course. 'I'm sure they were more than glad to be of service. Looks as if we'll be finishing on time today.'

Probably due to the fact that Sophie hadn't held the filming up once. She was grateful to Drew for not mentioning that. 'I'll be able to go and see Carly before dinner.'

He thought for a moment. 'Why don't I take you to the

hospital and then on to dinner? We could have a quiet meal somewhere, away from the hotel.'

That might not be as easy as it sounded. In Drew's world, you just walked into a restaurant, and if there was a spare table that was it. In hers, there was always a spare table, but with it went the complications of being recognised.

'I'd love it. Do you think we can find somewhere we won't be interrupted, though?' An image floated into her head. Lying on a beach, shaded by palm trees. Drew gently working the knots out of her spine, taking them one at a time. Not a bad analogy for the hundred small concerns that he seemed to have the solution for. Actually, not a bad daydream to have, just for the sake of it. Since it was a beach, and all in her mind anyway, it was entirely up to her what he was or, more to the point, wasn't wearing.

'If I can find somewhere out of the way…' He had obviously been applying himself to the problem in hand while she'd been daydreaming. 'How do you feel about motorbikes?'

Odd question. Sophie decided to go with the flow and work out what he was getting at later. 'My eldest brother had one. I used to love it.'

'So you've ridden pillion before?'

'Yes, all the time.'

'In that case, we could take my bike if you like. It's a lot easier to find somewhere quiet than having to cruise around in a taxi.' His eyes became serious. 'You'll be quite safe.'

'You have a motorbike?'

'Yeah, in the hotel car park.'

She'd seen it. A black and chrome machine that generally attracted a second glance from any of the men who happened to be passing. It had attracted a few second glances from her as well.

'Sounds great.' She put the beach image away for another time. She now had a new one to remind her that she was going out with Drew tonight.

CHAPTER SEVEN

DREW KNOCKED ON her hotel room door at exactly five o'clock. Sophie had been sitting on the bed, waiting.

He was all she'd hoped for, in a thick black leather jacket that somehow made his hair seem darker and his eyes a softer grey by contrast. Sophie swallowed hard.

His assessing gaze looked her up and down. She'd reckoned that jeans and a pair of ankle boots would be most appropriate, and had thrown in the pink lacy top just for fun.

'You'll need a jacket…' His gaze travelled over her bare arms, and Sophie shivered.

'Will this do?' She held out the thick waterproof jacket that she usually kept in her trailer for night shoots.

His fingers brushed the material of the sleeve. 'That'll be fine.'

Drew turned abruptly, leading the way down to the hotel car park, and Sophie wondered whether he was having second thoughts. Maybe the pink top had been too frivolous. He obviously took his bike pretty seriously.

'We could still get a taxi.'

He nodded. 'Whatever you prefer. If you don't fancy the bike…'

It would have been easier to have shrugged and left the decision to him, as if she didn't care one way or the other. Sophie took a breath. Mentally walking away was just as bad as physically walking away. 'Are you thinking that I'm worried about being safe?'

A glint of relief showed in his eyes. 'Yeah. It's not that long since you were injured in an accident.'

'I'd rather be in your hands than those of a crazy minicab driver.' Sophie felt herself blush. Maybe she could have phrased that a little better. 'Anyway, most real bike riders I know are pretty hot on safety. And this does look like a real bike.'

She grinned at him, running her hand appreciatively across the leather saddle, and he smiled. 'Yeah. All right. Careful of my ego, it'll explode in a minute.'

He rather unnecessarily checked that her jacket was firmly zipped up and the helmet strapped firmly under her chin. Sophie let him do it. The brush of his fingers on her neck might be businesslike, but it still made her shiver with pleasure. He swung his leg over the bike, settling himself in the saddle, and she took hold of his shoulder to steady herself as she climbed on behind him.

'Put your feet on there…that's right.' He was acting as if she'd never ridden a motorbike before. 'And watch out for the exhaust, it gets hot.'

'Got it. Piranhas again.' Little biking piranhas this time, with motorcycle helmets and big teeth.

He chuckled. 'Yeah.'

Drew put his helmet on and reached back, taking hold of her gloved hands and pulling them around his waist. She held onto him, relaxing against him, feeling the pliable strength of his body. She'd known all along that this was going to be the very best part of the trip.

A few turns around the car park seemed to satisfy him that she was confident enough for the open road. On the back of a large, heavy bike like this one a pillion rider had to go with the flow, following the movements of the driver. This seemed like a marvellous adventure, riding with him, trusting him to keep her safe. Sophie hadn't reckoned on trusting any man to do that in the foreseeable future.

When they arrived at the hospital, Carly put the lid on her exhilaration. She subjected Drew to ten minutes of rigorous questioning and a couple of stern exhortations as to the need for absolute discretion, which prompted urgent gestures to *cut* from Sophie, from behind his back. Then she relaxed against her pillows and professed herself glad to see them both.

'She seems to be doing well.' They were strolling through the hospital car park to where they'd left his bike.

'Yeah. If she can manage to divert some of that determination of hers to getting better, and not worrying about everyone else, she'll be out tomorrow.' Drew had good-humouredly said as much to Carly. 'Then we inherit the problem of finding a way of getting her to rest. She really shouldn't just get up and start work again straight away. She needs to take things very easy for a couple of weeks.'

'I think I've got the solution to that.' Sophie grinned smugly. It was nice to have a solution rather than be the problem for a change.

'What are you intending doing? Sedating her and tying her to the bed? I might be able to help with the sedation…'

'That's my second option. The first one's better. I emailed her husband, Mark, and he can fly over to fetch her in a couple of days. He'll take her home to recuperate.'

He chuckled. 'Passing the problem over to him, huh? Sounds like a tremendous idea.'

'Glad you like it. Mark will drive down here, spend the night and then take Carly back with him the next day, in time for their flight in the afternoon.'

'It's a lot of travelling. Would it be better if I hired a car and drove Carly up to London? They could spend the night in a hotel and then fly back the following day, it would be easier on them both.'

'Would you?' Sophie had thought of that, but not known how to ask. Drew had already done so much. 'I don't dare take another day off filming. I've been trying Joel's patience enough already.'

'Leave it with me. If you let me have Mark's email address I'll contact him and sort the details out.'

'I...' Sophie pressed her lips together.

'You what?' He grinned.

'I told Mark to leave the flights and the hotel to me. I want her to be comfortable, so I was thinking first-class tickets.'

'That's nice of you. So you'll arrange the flights and the hotel, and I'll do the driving, then.'

'You trust me?' After all the slips, all the lapses in memory, he had every reason not to. Sophie had only just got to grips with Drew's full name.

'You're just as capable of making a couple of phone calls as I am. Write a list and tick everything off. That's what most people do.' There was a hint of humour in his eyes.

'Okay. Deal.' Sophie pulled her notebook from her bag, and Drew waited while she wrote a note to herself. 'Are we going for something to eat now? I'm hungry.'

She didn't ask where they were going. Sophie submitted to the ritual of having him check that her helmet was on correctly, and climbed onto the seat behind him. Melting with him into the anonymity of two riders, who stopped at an organic burger stall then headed out of town.

They were free. Away from everyone and everything. There were too many layers of clothing between them to feel his body, but his solidity, his strength were there. Sophie thrilled at the way he pushed her a little, opening up the throttle slowly until she clung to him much tighter than she really needed to.

He turned into empty country lanes and then again onto a dirt track. The bike climbed the steep pathway, winding through a copse of trees, and then suddenly the horizon opened up in a wide panorama. They were on a clifftop, the sea thirty feet below them, the sky above them. Nothing else but a few gulls, wheeling above them.

'Wow!' She took her helmet off, shaking her hair out into the breeze, her legs still trembling from the exhilaration of riding with him. Drew manoeuvred the bike off the track and swung out of the saddle, taking the foil-wrapped packages from the pannier.

'These smell good.' He investigated the contents of one. 'And they're still hot.'

Sophie sat down on the grass beside the bike. 'How did you find that place?'

'I asked at the hospital. Nurses always know where to get the best takeaways in town.' He grinned, sitting down next to her. 'Is this okay?'

That could mean one of many things. Are *you* okay? Is *this* okay? He probably meant all of them, and Sophie decided to answer all of them.

'Yes. It's great.'

It had been sheer self-indulgence on his part. Having her ride with him on the back of the bike, bringing her out here where they could be alone, was the stuff that dreams were made of. His dreams, at any rate.

And she was enjoying herself. She seemed to visibly relax, to give up the constant struggle to remember, the constant search for things she may have forgotten. Drew told himself that this had been the real plan all along.

'Do you want to walk a bit? There's a path down to the beach a couple of miles along here.' Every one of his senses was putting in urgent requests for this evening to last as long as possible.

'Sounds great. I could do with a walk, blow the cobwebs away.'

She clung to him as he manoeuvred the bike back onto

the track, her arms clasped tightly around his waist. This felt too good to question, too good to do anything other than enjoy it while he could, because it wasn't going to last for ever. Following the curve of the coastline, he drove towards the steps, which led down to sea level, and a sheltered beach.

There was no particular need to help her down the steps, but he did so anyway. Sophie didn't seem to mind, and it was just one more thing that added to the magic. They walked slowly in the gathering dusk, and Drew searched the sky, looking for the first glimmer of an evening star.

'Can I ask you something?'

'Of course. What do you want to know?'

'The things I've forgotten. Do you think they'll ever come back again?'

Perhaps this was the real nature of the bargain. Someone as beautiful as Sophie, who had everything going for her apart from this one thing, probably wouldn't have given him the time of day if she hadn't needed him so badly. He forced his mind away from evening stars and all the things that they seemed to represent at the moment.

'I think you have to prepare for the fact that there are some things you'll never remember.'

'But…' She slipped her hand into the crook of his arm, hanging onto him tightly. 'I'd try anything. Drugs, meditation. What about hypnotism?'

'Like in the films? Someone goes to a hypnotist and remembers every detail of something they didn't know about before?' He took the risk of chiding her gently and she shrugged, giving a little laugh.

'It's so important to me, Drew.'

He was blinded for a moment, lost in the sheer delight that this was the first time she'd called him by his first name without having to think about it. Drew reminded himself that he ought to be concentrating on the rest of what she was saying.

'I'm sorry, but it doesn't work that way, Sophie. In a lot

of cases like yours, it's not the ability to retrieve memories that's impaired but the process by which events are written into the memory in the first place. If something isn't there, it can't be retrieved.'

'So there's no hope?' She gave a little gesture of frustration with her free hand.

'I think that pinning your hopes on the future would be more productive. How you can improve things now.'

A huff of disappointment escaped her lips. They walked in silence, Sophie seemingly lost in her own thoughts.

'Does it matter so very much to you, Sophie?' It seemed that the past was more important than either the present or the future to her at the moment.

'Yes. It does.'

'Is it the accident? It's very common for people who've been injured in accidents not to be able to remember.'

'Partly. I was driving and the car ran off the road and into a tree.' She gave a little shrug. 'Since it wasn't the tree's fault, I guess it must have been mine.'

Something about the way she was clinging to him told Drew that there was more to it than that. 'And there are other things?'

'Yeah. I don't remember very much about the fortnight afterwards either. What I did…' She sighed. 'Have you ever begged someone to tell you the truth?'

'Yeah.' Sophie looked as surprised as Drew felt at his admission. 'A woman. I begged her to tell me the truth, and she said that I was crazy. That everything my common sense was telling me was a lie.'

'Does it still hurt?'

'No. It was a long time ago.' What Gina had done didn't hurt any more. It had just made Drew more wary, convinced him that most things that glittered weren't gold. And that included the world that Sophie inhabited.

She tipped her face up towards him, and suddenly it felt

as if her gaze really was golden. 'I begged, too. And Josh told me I was crazy. Only I can't remember...'

'Tell me about it.'

She seemed about to say something and then turned her head away, looking out to sea. The evening breeze swirled around them, seeming to snatch the moment away.

Drew hung onto it doggedly. 'Tell me, Sophie. I won't tell you that you're crazy.'

'There's not that much to tell. I met Josh on set when I was making my last film. He had a smallish part.' She shrugged. 'Very small, actually. Everyone said that he cared about my fame a bit more than he cared about me, but I didn't listen. There was something about him and I thought he loved me.'

'But?' Sophie raised an eyebrow, and Drew shrugged. 'There's always a *but*.'

'I'd like to think not. But... When I got this film he demanded that I only take it on condition that he got the male lead. He wasn't right for it, and even if he had been, that's not something that I have the power to do. So he dumped me.'

'Because you couldn't further his career.'

'Yeah. More or less. But then, while I was here last winter, he got in touch again. Said he wanted me to take him back, and when I went back to the States...I did. He walked the red carpets with me, got the column inches. But that was all it was to him. I could see that by then.'

'So you left him.'

The sadness in Sophie's sigh made his heart lurch. 'I was going to tell him. But he asked me to go away with him for a couple of weeks, see if we could work things out, and I went. That was when I crashed the car. He wasn't injured, and we went on to the hotel after the hospital discharged us.'

'And you don't remember any of that?'

'Not much. I remember going back to Los Angeles on my own. Then three weeks later the stories started to hit the newsstands. He'd sold his story. I think he got quite a lot for it, but there was spite in there as well. How he was the guy who went out with a bad girl who broke his heart. That's when all the rumours started about my drinking.'

'He made it up?'

'He said I'd been drinking when I crashed the car, and somehow managed to get out of being breathalysed. I don't know whether that's true or not.'

It was then that it hit Drew. As if a massive, freak wave had rolled in from the sea, engulfing him and leaving him struggling for breath. Some events defined you in life. Sophie couldn't remember those all-important moments, so she couldn't remember who she really was.

'Sophie…' He wanted to give her some comfort, throw her something to hang onto, but he had nothing. For all his arsenal of coping strategies and carefully thought-through responses, there was nothing that could deal with this.

'It doesn't matter. If I can't remember, that's an end to it.' She was moving onto the defensive now.

'So what, then? You're just going to give up?'

She pulled her hand from the crook of his arm, roughly. 'You think I'm giving up? Look again.' Sophie began to walk down to the water's edge, as if plunging into the sea was the only way that she could get away from all of this.

'Don't walk away from me, Sophie.'

When she turned, she was trembling. 'You just told me it was no use. If I can't remember then so be it, there's nothing more to say.'

'There's plenty more. Like going to see a specialist, being properly diagnosed. Getting some help with the here and now. Coping strategies…'

She held up her hand to stop him. 'All right. You've said it once, and I heard and wrote it down. I'm thinking about it.'

'And what are you doing in the meantime? Wearing a tin-foil hat to bed?'

'Fine doctor you are. You think bullying your patients is the way to go?'

She was right. One hundred per cent. This was no way to

treat a patient, taking them out into the middle of nowhere and arguing with them. 'You're not my patient.'

'Maybe you should wear a sign. *The doctor is in. The doctor is out.* I'm beginning to lose track…'

She was suddenly silent as he took her by the shoulders. Looking up at him, her lips parted slightly, almost as if she expected him to shake some sense into her, somehow wanted him to.

'The doctor's out right now Sophie. And I'm telling you now that if you don't agree to go and see someone and get your condition properly diagnosed, I'm going to throw you over my shoulder and carry you there.'

'Really?' There was a strange light in her eyes. Almost as if she'd been waiting for him to finally break and say something like this. 'That's not very sympathetic.'

'It's not meant to be. Sympathy can't change what's happened. You deserve to have a different future.'

'I want a different future.' She seemed to be mulling the idea over. 'You'll suggest someone?'

'Yeah. I can do that.'

'Okay. You tell me where to go, and I'll go.'

All he could think about was her face, tipped up towards him in the gathering gloom. And all he wanted to do was kiss her, but that was a bad idea. Drew contented himself with taking her arm in his again. The first stars were appearing in a violet sky, and for the moment it was more than enough to be able to walk with her under their meagre light.

CHAPTER EIGHT

A CAR ACCIDENT. An ex-partner who had clearly done something but she couldn't remember exactly what. It was little enough to go on. The irony of the situation didn't escape him. He had to do just what Sophie did every day, piecing the truth together from disparate half-remembered clues.

He stowed one of the motorcycle helmets away in the back of the wardrobe, leaving the other one on the bed. Despite his own best resolutions to leave it alone, he couldn't help wondering, nagging away at the problem. Maybe he'd go out again, ride for as long as it took to clear his head.

That wasn't going to work. Drew had the feeling that he could drive halfway across Europe and back, and it still wouldn't be far enough for him to come to any conclusion at all. He fell asleep in the armchair in the corner of his room, waking to the sound of his phone.

'Charlie? What's up?' He tucked the phone against his shoulder, trying to massage some feeling back into his cramped arm.

'Are you alone?'

'Yeah, of course. It's six in the morning.'

'Just asking. Have you seen the papers yet?'

'No.' Something about Charlie's tone indicated that this wasn't just an idle question. 'Should I have done?'

'Apparently Sophie Warner's got a new mystery man.'

'What?' This had to be another lie. Sophie had spent almost all of her time in the last few days with him. When had she even had time for a mystery man?

'There's a picture in this morning's paper of her perched on your bike. Holding a motorcycle helmet and looking pretty stunning, actually.'

'Me?'

'Yeah, you. I'd recognise your bike anywhere. Wake up, will you?'

Drew was wide awake now. Sophie had waited with the bike when he'd gone to get the burgers yesterday evening. She'd taken her helmet off… 'Are there any of me?' A sudden, irrational sense of dread engulfed him.

'There's another one of the two of you riding off. But you can't see who it is she's with. You've both got your helmets on. So what's the story?'

'I gave her a lift, that's all. Carly's in hospital—'

'Really? Is she all right?'

'Yeah, she's fine. Appendicitis. They operated the night before last and she's already sitting up in bed and arguing with everyone.' For once, Drew's mind wasn't on the medical details. He was wondering whether there was any way that his prospective employers would see the photographs and identify him from them.

'Where is she? I'll send her some flowers.'

'She's probably going to be coming back here today.' Drew couldn't work up much enthusiasm for Carly's flowers either. 'Can you actually…see my face?'

'In the photos? Nah. Like I said, I recognised the bike.'

That was something, at least. No publicity was bad publicity in Sophie's world, and she could ride around with as many mystery men as she liked. But it was unlikely that being associated with a film star who had a reputation for bad behaviour could do Drew's medical career all that much good.

Suddenly he was ashamed of the thought. The lies and half-truths in the press gave Sophie enough pain already, without him adding to it all by being ashamed to be seen with her. 'Charlie, would you do me a favour?'

'Fire away.'

'If you happen to run across anyone who has any media influence, perhaps you could mention that…' Drew thought better of the idea. The media was a complex and dangerous animal, and he was beginning to realise how little he understood it.

Charlie came to his rescue.

'I guess that since you're still there, and you've taken the lady for a ride on your precious bike, she's not as bad as she's painted.'

'No, she isn't. Not at all.'

'But you can't talk about it?'

'No. I can't. Confidentiality agreement.'

Charlie chortled. 'Okay. I get it. Look, the best thing that you can do is to get her to talk to her media people, give them something concrete to back up her side of the story.'

'Okay.' Sophie was never going to agree to that. 'Thanks.'

'No problem. Call me if you need me. I got you into this…'

'Nah. I got myself into this one.' Drew squinted at the clock and decided that he had some more time. 'So what have you been up to?'

'Bit of this, bit of that…'

Drew grinned. That generally meant that Charlie's ever restless attention had been caught by something that interested him. 'Bit of what?' He stood up to stretch, and then flopped down onto the bed, lying on his back, looking at the ceiling. He had another half-hour before he needed to get into the shower and then go and wake Sophie.

She'd woken him. Drew had finished his call with Charlie and then fallen asleep on the bed. The next he knew was that Sophie was hammering on the door and when he opened it she was wearing a smile that said that she rather liked switching roles with him once in a while.

After a slightly shaky start, the day gradually turned into a success. No one seemed much interested in the papers, and when Sophie found Drew studying the pictures, she twisted the edges of her mouth down and then shrugged helplessly. The whole set was beginning to relax now, and Joel seemed anxious to keep it that way, making sure that he bumped into Drew at least three times in the course of the day, asking him each time if everything was okay with Sophie.

They returned to the hotel to find that Carly was out of hospital. Sophie went straight upstairs to see her, and Drew gave them half an hour alone together before he popped his head around the open door of Sophie's suite, knocking as he did so.

Carly was lying propped up on the sofa, obviously in fighting form. 'No, Soph, it sounds like a pretty bad idea to me.'

'No, it's not.' Both faces swung round towards Drew as they heard him by the door.

'I'll…come back later.' If they were in the middle of an argument, Drew didn't want to intrude.

'No, that's okay. Come in.' Sophie shot him a *please stay* look, while Carly's face hardened into a *just go* stare. Drew pretended not to notice either of them and gave Carly his most innocent smile.

'You're looking better, Carly.'

'See.' Apparently he'd just provided Carly with a piece of ammunition to hurl at Sophie.

'I…hope you're resting up.'

Apparently that redressed the balance. Sophie shot Carly an *I told you so* look.

The two of them seemed at an impasse. What was it Charlie always said? Never get between the girl you fancy and her best friend. Drew wondered whether his status as a doctor would protect him a little from the consequences of breaking that apparently sensible rule, and realised that he couldn't hide behind that whenever it suited him.

'Your shoulder hurts?' Drew noticed that Carly was absently rubbing her right shoulder.

'Yeah, a bit. I must have been lying on it.'

'Not necessarily. They pump gas into your abdomen to do the laparoscopy. It can cause you pain for a little while afterwards.'

Carly frowned. 'I've got gas? In my shoulder?'

'No. It's probably referred pain from your diaphragm. I don't suppose you told your doctor about this at the hospital?'

'I didn't think it was relevant.'

Sophie rolled her eyes. 'You're supposed to tell the doctor what your symptoms are and let him decide what's relevant.'

He shot her a grin, wondering if she remembered who she'd got those words from. Sophie's slight shrug told him that she was owning up to nothing.

'I imagine the doctor said you should walk around a bit, as soon as you feel able.' He fixed Carly with what he hoped was a no-nonsense look.

'Yeah. And I will be walking around. I'll be getting back to work soon.'

'Walking about a bit is not the same as being on your feet for sixteen hours a day. Did you think to mention that your job isn't exactly a nine to five?' Drew had seen how hard everyone on the set worked. Early mornings, evening shoots, night shoots. It was relentless.

Carly didn't reply to his question, so Sophie provided the answer. 'Obviously not. You need a bit of time to recuperate, and I've been on the phone to Mark. He'll be here in a couple of days to take you home.'

A tear glistened in the corner of Carly's eye. 'But, Soph… What about you?'

'I'm fine. Drew's been helping me, and I'm going to see a doctor that he knows. I feel much better, just knowing that

I'm doing something, and that there's a lot more that I can do. You're best off at home with Mark and I'm best off here.'

Drew couldn't help grinning. The Sophie who spoke wasn't the one he'd first met, vague and temperamental. Her voice was firm and assertive, and she knew exactly what she wanted.

Carly frowned in Drew's direction and he shrugged. 'Don't drag me into this. I just do whatever I'm told.'

'I bet you do.' Carly folded her arms across her chest. 'All right. Have it your way. I never thought you'd turn into such a diva, Soph.'

Sophie laughed and hugged her friend. As Drew turned to leave them alone, he saw grateful tears glistening in Carly's eyes.

Sophie was proud of herself. She'd made a list, carefully ticking off each task as it was accomplished and making notes under each entry. It would have been easy—no, expected—that she would just have asked Jennie to do it but doing it herself had brought with it a feeling of power. A feeling that she could do these things if she tried.

The airline tickets were booked and Carly's husband was arriving in London in two days' time. He and Carly were booked into a hotel for the night, and the car was hired so that Drew could take Carly to London to meet him.

'Is that everything?' She pushed the piece of paper with her carefully transcribed notes across the breakfast table towards Drew.

He scanned it carefully. 'Looks like it. I have something for you.' He passed a business card to her.

'Dr Henry Chancellor.' She whispered the name quietly. It seemed almost like a magic spell.

'Yeah. I've spoken to his secretary. I didn't give your name, but he's going to make himself available for an appointment at short notice.'

'I don't know when—'

'You can come to London with Carly and me.'

It all seemed so sudden. So soon. 'But...I don't think I can make it, Drew. The filming schedule. Like I said, I don't want to mess Joel around any more than I already have.'

'I spoke to Joel. He's happy to reschedule to give you a couple of days off to come to London with us.'

'You did...what?' Sophie got to her feet and then sank back down into her chair. She didn't do that any more, she didn't run. She stayed and fought. 'You promised me, Drew.'

'I didn't tell him anything. He mentioned to me that you might want to go down to London to see Carly off, and I said I thought it would be a good idea.'

'Joel never *just* mentions anything.'

'Well, maybe I just happened to mention to him that we were going...' Drew had a look of studied innocence on his face, and the conversation clearly hadn't been as casual as he was making out.

'Come on, Drew. I'm paying you the respect of not walking away, so perhaps you can return the favour and give it to me straight.'

'Okay. You've got a point. Joel knows that something's going on, and he realises that it's being sorted. He hasn't pushed me for any details, and if he's willing to give you a bit of space without asking why, then I think you should take it.'

'And what *did* you say to him?'

'Just that I'd have you back on Saturday evening, ready for work on Sunday.'

'And that's what you intend to do?'

Drew grinned at her. 'That's exactly what I intend to do.'

It sounded like a plan. Now that she had the card in her hand, it sounded like a very good plan. 'So you'll call your friend?'

He chuckled. 'What, too much of a diva to make a phone call for yourself?'

'Don't make fun of me.'

His face was suddenly tender. 'I'm sorry. It's up to you, though, to make a time you feel comfortable with and to ask any questions that you want to ask when you make the appointment.' He took the card from her hand, writing on the back of it.

'Speak to Molly, Henry's secretary. He may well want to have an MRI scan done on the Friday, and see you to discuss the results on the Saturday. Is that okay?'

'Yes. It's good.' Sophie reached into her handbag for her notebook, and slipped the card between the pages. 'Shall I make a booking at the hotel?'

'For yourself, if you want. My place is in London, so I'll go back there and pick up my post. And if it's not too humble for a diva to stay overnight…?' He ducked back, as Sophie swatted the notebook in his direction.

'Mark and Carly aren't going to need me hanging around. And I think I can rough it for one night.'

CHAPTER NINE

'I'M SCARED, DREW.'

Everything had gone without a hitch so far. They had driven from Devon to London early that morning, and Mark had been waiting for Carly at the hotel. Hugs and kisses were exchanged, and then Drew drove Sophie to a private hospital in Harley Street, using the car park under the building and hustling her straight into the lift.

She was booked in for a MRI scan as Sophie DeAngelo and had reminded Drew to give her a nudge if she failed to respond to the name. Now came what felt like the scariest bit of the whole weekend.

'I'm *really scared.*' She picked up a magazine from the table in the private waiting room, flipping through it without reading anything. 'What if I panic in the machine? People do, you know.'

'Yeah, sometimes. But it's not the end of the world if you do. And you've already been through a lot worse, and held your nerve.' He laid his hand on hers, and she realised that she had been shredding the pages of the magazine between her fingers. 'Stop that. You're tearing me in half.'

Sophie focussed on the glossy paper. Drew's smile sparkled up at her, despite her having ripped one of his ears off. She smoothed the page, reading the heading of the article.

Dr Drew Taylor talks about the diagnosis and treatment of brain injuries.

'I might have to retract a couple of things I said in the article. In the light of recent experience.' He was grinning.

'Why?'

'Because I said that early diagnosis and therapy is vital. That was before I met an actress who decided she didn't need either of those things, and still managed to keep working.'

'I haven't exactly been at my best.'

'Well, maybe I'll just leave that bit in, then.'

'Why didn't you say something about this?' Sophie flipped to the cover of the magazine. It was a serious, well-regarded publication, aimed at educating lay people about medical matters.

'I didn't think you much liked guys who wrote magazine articles…' His lips twitched in wry humour and when Sophie started to laugh he grinned.

'Idiot. This couldn't be more different. Do you think they'd mind if I took this home to read?'

'I imagine they'll insist on it, now that you've torn it to pieces. They've probably got a few of them, they're good to put in the waiting room.'

Sophie slipped the magazine into her bag. 'I'll give the receptionist the money for it.'

'If you must. Now, what were we saying? About you panicking?'

'I can't remember.' Suddenly she felt safe. She was with Drew, and nothing bad was going to happen.

They waited another five minutes, then a nurse showed her to a small cubicle, and Sophie undressed, folding her clothes carefully. Drew was waiting for her outside and walked with her into the stark, white-painted room that housed the scanner.

'Sit up here.' He laid his hand on the long padded bench in front of the machine. It looked as if it was about to eat her.

'It's big, isn't it?'

'Yeah. It'll be a bit noisy when it gets going as well, but that's nothing to worry about. I'll be through there, and I'll be watching you all the time.' He took her hand in his, smiling down at her. 'It'll be over before you know it.'

A pinprick in her arm, which she hardly felt, because she was looking at Drew. A technician positioned her head, and a doctor took Drew to one side for a few words. Then he had to go.

He brushed his fingers against hers, told her that everything was going to be okay and walked away. Then the technician's voice over the intercom, quiet and reassuring, telling her when to breathe in, when to hold her breath…

Then it was over. The nurse helped her up from the bench and she changed back into her clothes, her hands shaking with relief.

'Did you see the results?' She found Drew pacing restlessly outside and caught at the fabric of his sleeve. Someone had said something about results, she was sure of it.

'The results need to be analysed by computer first. Henry Chancellor will have them tomorrow, and when you go and see him he'll explain everything to you.'

'Okay. Thanks. Can we go now, then?'

'All right.' Winding his arm around her shoulder, he guided her towards the lift.

Downstairs, he put the keys into the ignition of the hire car and left them there untouched, turning to face her. 'I was thinking we might go somewhere tonight.' He shot her a mouthwatering smile.

He was keeping her busy, trying to stop her from fretting about tomorrow. It was an obvious ruse, and it seemed to be working. 'Did you have anywhere in mind?'

'Not really. I thought we could go to my place, book somewhere quiet and go out for a meal. Catch the cinema if we felt like it.'

A tingle ran down Sophie's spine. She knew an opportunity when she ran across it, and this felt like one. She'd been passing her opportunities by for too many months now, just drifting in a world where nothing made sense to her.

'I've got a better idea. Let's go out somewhere bright, and noisy and full of people having fun.'

He grinned. 'Yeah?'

'Don't you like the idea?'

'What's not to like? A gorgeous movie star on my arm for the night.'

'A minor movie star…'

'If you say so.' He didn't seem to bother much about the intricate hierarchies of fame. 'We can get my old banger out of the garage, give her a run. She gets a bit choked up when I don't drive her for a while.'

'An old banger?' Sophie couldn't imagine Drew driving an old banger of a car. He liked anything mechanical far too much for that.

'Well…' His grey eyes glinted. 'She's sleek, beautiful. Smells nice. But she is a little temperamental at times. It's nothing I can't handle.'

'Your ideal woman, then.'

'Well, she doesn't have much of a sense of humour.' He chuckled as if that was a private joke between a man and his car. 'What do you think?'

That sounded like a challenge. And Sophie wasn't going to be upstaged by a car. 'We'd have to do it properly.'

'Yeah? What do you suggest?'

She took the opportunity to look him up and down, imagining him darkly handsome in a dinner suit. 'I need a dress. A really nice one…'

Something ignited in his eyes. He liked the idea. A lot. And Sophie knew that this was something she could do for him. Probably better than Drew could imagine.

It was almost surreal. Sophie had made a phone call and given his address. By the time they got home, a courier was waiting on the doorstep with half a dozen large boxes. He helped her carry them up to the spare room and stacked them next to the wardrobe, and then she'd shooed him away, without giving any hint of what they contained.

The silence in the house for the next thirty minutes indicated that Sophie had done as he'd suggested, and lain down for a nap. When Drew heard the noise of the shower from upstairs, he changed into his best suit and waited.

An hour later, he was sitting in the lounge, trying to pin his attention on the pages of a book, but actually wondering whether a black hole had opened up in his house and she'd fallen into it. A noise at the doorway grabbed his attention.

Wow. Just…*wow*.

By some unknown process that defied medical principles, blood rushed simultaneously to his head and down to another part of his body that he'd been trying to ignore for the last two weeks. Sophie had pulled out all of the stops this time, and the transformation made him want to fall to his knees.

She glittered…no, she shimmered…in a dark blue sequinned dress that clung to her curves, high-heeled silver sandals, which made her legs look impossibly long, and a small silver and blue clutch bag. Her hair was done in a gravity-defying arrangement of curls, which framed her face perfectly.

'You look…' Words failed him.

She smiled and a bright shiver ran down his spine. 'Is that good speechless, or bad speechless?' She knew exactly what effect she was having on him, and it seemed that was exactly what she'd wanted.

'Good. Definitely good speechless.' Confounded as he was by her magic, Drew still couldn't quite square the mathematics of six boxes and only one dress. 'So what did your fairy godmother put in the other boxes?'

'I had a choice of dresses.' She giggled at his obvious confusion. 'Designers lend things out all the time. It's good publicity for them if a celebrity wears their latest creation.'

A sudden desire to see her in all six was quenched by the thought that she looked just perfect, and he wouldn't change a thing. He rose, pulling his jacket on, and she smiled, looking him up and down unashamedly.

'You scrub up pretty well too, Drew Taylor.'

It still gave him a thrill whenever he heard his name on her lips. He wondered if she'd used it because she knew…

'I'm still getting used to seeing the many faces of Sophie Warner.' At first it had unnerved Drew that she seemed to be able to slip from one character to another so easily. But this was completely different. She wasn't trying to beguile him, or pull the wool over his eyes. She'd done this for him. To give him pleasure.

'Do you mind my many faces?'

'I find them endlessly entrancing. And having you on my arm tonight is the best gift you could give me.'

She nodded, as if she'd got the answer she wanted, walking over to him and slipping her hand into the crook of his elbow. This he was going to enjoy.

Drew's sitting-room was warm and welcoming, filled with books and photographs, a feeling of space and light. A pair of vintage red leather chairs matched the throw, slung across the back of a modern sofa. It put the carefully designed interiors of the faceless homes that Sophie had rented of late to shame. This was all about comfort, individuality and effortless style.

The garage lay on the ground floor of the three storey house and she followed him downstairs with a little thrill of anticipation, blinking as he switched on the lights. It was white painted, orderly, with a space for his bike. And a small, neat sports car.

'She's beautiful, Drew. Fabulous…'

'You like her?' he asked with a smile. 'I hope she doesn't get the sulks.'

'Why would she do that?' Drew had obviously lavished a

great deal of care on the car. The opalescent grey paintwork gleamed. Through the window, she could see a fifties-style dashboard and cream leather seats.

'She's used to being the most beautiful thing in this garage. You've just changed all that.'

Yes! She'd gone out to wow him, and she'd obviously succeeded. Sophie shivered with pleasure.

'Thank you. How old…? What year is she?' It probably wasn't a good idea to ask the lady's age.

'Nineteen fifty-seven. When I got her she was just a rusted chassis. Took me six years to rebuild.'

'And you painted her to match your eyes?' She couldn't resist teasing him a little.

He opened the passenger door, grinning. 'That wasn't my thought at the time.'

It was tricky getting into the low seat with such high heels, but Drew's arm was there to steady her. When he slid into the driver's seat, the look on his face made her heart turn over. Pure enjoyment. And she was a part of it. He'd wanted to share his most treasured possession with her, and he'd said that she was *more* beautiful. Sophie sent a mental apology to the little car, and hoped it understood that this was a special night for her.

'Ready to go?' He grinned at her, darkly handsome.

'Yes.' She was ready for anything tonight.

He'd chosen a West End theatreland restaurant for cocktails and then dinner. The maître d' recognised Sophie and tried to usher her to a better table than the one that Drew had been able to procure, but she waved him away.

'Don't you want to sit over there?' Drew nodded towards the table she'd been offered, close to the piano.

'Not particularly. They always want you to sit somewhere that people can see you. I'm not here for that tonight.'

'What about the dress? Doesn't your designer want some photos in the morning paper?' It would be good to know when to expect a camera lens, so he could melt quietly into the background.

'I told him tonight was a private engagement. I've worn plenty of his stuff on the red carpet and he's happy to do me a few favours in return once in a while.'

The small, circular table in the corner of the restaurant suddenly became Drew's whole world. This was for him. Not the cameras, or the publicity people. All for him.

'Would you like a cocktail?'

She turned the shimmer of her smile onto him, and he almost blinked in its brilliance. 'Yes, I'd love one.' She picked the cocktail menu up from the table and held it up in front of her face, peering over the top of it at the bustle and noise around her. Only Drew could see the curve of her red lips. 'This is fun, isn't it?'

The service was a great deal better than he was used to and the meal was excellent. When an elaborately arranged confection was placed in front of her for sweet, she leaned towards him confidingly.

'I think the people at the next table have just recognised you...'

Drew chuckled. 'You mean they've recognised you.' He was pretty sure that he didn't warrant this kind of attention.

'Maybe. Although you're much more useful to have around.'

'What makes you say that?' Drew couldn't imagine that he could be more important than Sophie in the eyes of the people around them. He was just a dark suit, which served only to emphasise her gleam.

'If someone were to be ill...' she said, looking around, as if checking that everyone within view seemed healthy '...you'd go and do your thing.'

'I suppose so.' Drew hoped fervently that no one at a nearby table was going to use this moment to collapse. 'It would depend...'

'Depend on what?' Her gaze was on him now, making him shiver.

'Well, if someone cut their finger, I might just leave them to it.'

'And if someone had a heart attack?'

'If someone had a heart attack, I'd wish they'd chosen another time, but…' Drew shrugged '… I'd have to go.'

'Yes. My father was a doctor. Did I mention that?'

That little quirk of her lips again. Drew probed gently. 'I guess he wasn't always around, then.'

'He was never around. Not like you.'

Drew ignored the obvious unfairness of the statement. He'd been accused of being never around enough times to know that he was no angel in that department. And he knew that he couldn't change. 'Have you told your family about the difficulties you've been having?'

'No.'

'Don't you think they might want to know?'

She shrugged, the shimmer of her dress sparkling suddenly. 'My mum and dad are abroad. Dad works for a medical aid agency. I know what he'd say…'

'What's that?'

'He'd say that he can't get away at the moment.' She looked up at him, wrinkling her nose slightly. 'I'm the black sheep of the family.'

'Really? Surely they're proud of your success.'

'To my dad it's all Hollywood nonsense. My two older brothers both followed in the family footsteps and became doctors. He reckons that they're the ones who are doing something useful with their lives.'

At one time Drew might have unthinkingly agreed with that. That had been before he'd really got to know Sophie.

'I suppose your father thinks that medicine is all about what *he* does.'

'I don't understand.'

'Doctors can only do so much. We can diagnose, and

often we can treat. We rely on people like you to give our patients the will to keep going.'

She narrowed her eyes. 'That's a generous thing to say. I'm not sure that anything I've done gives anyone the will to keep going.'

'Not on your own maybe. But never underestimate the power of a smile to make someone feel better. And that's your territory, not mine.'

'You want to try telling my father that?' She grinned at him, obviously pleased with the idea.

'No. I think you might, though.'

She shook her head. 'I need all my wits about me for that kind of discussion.'

'Then that's one hell of a good reason for you to work on getting better.'

'Okay. Remind me to write that down when we get back to your place. My notebook wouldn't fit in this evening bag.' Suddenly her gaze was on his face. 'I'd like to know something.'

Drew could tell that the something mattered to her. 'What do you want to know?'

'It's your job to look after me, I know that. Everyone wants me to come up with the goods, to get this film finished...'

Drew had been telling himself the same thing. But he couldn't pretend any more. Sophie herself was far more interesting to him than any medical condition she could possibly contrive to manifest.

'Soph... I look at you, and I see...' He shrugged. 'What I don't see is a traumatic brain injury, or a case of heterochromia. I see a strong, beautiful woman, with eyes that fascinate me. I don't want to be your doctor, or your minder, and getting the film made isn't that high on my list of priorities.'

Her smile radiated through the space between them, seeming to light up the room. 'What is high on your list of priorities?'

'Right now? Asking you to dance with me comes in as the clear favourite.' He nodded towards the piano at the far end of the restaurant, where people were dancing to a slow, lilting melody.

She smiled, holding out her hand, and he rose, hardly able to believe his good fortune. Drew led her through the maze of tables, aware that all eyes were on them, and not caring. For tonight, at least, he felt like the luckiest man in London.

They'd danced, gone back to their table for coffee, and then danced again. It was heaven. Feeling his body against hers, strong and graceful. His smile, his scent.

He was every birthday, every Christmas that her father hadn't been there rolled up into one. All the bad decisions she'd made in her life, and all the good ones, everything she'd remembered and forgotten, they all seemed to have led up to this night. She was playing the fairy-tale princess, and he filled the part of her Prince Charming so very well.

Drew paid the bill, brushing away the manager's protests that their meal was on the house. The car was on a meter a little way along the road, but instead they walked, finding themselves on the Embankment, the Thames glittering darkly on one side of them and the bright lights of the city on the other.

'What are you going to do next?' Sophie had been too busy trying to push Drew away to bother with that up till now.

'I've got a job that starts in two and a half months. Director of a memory clinic, here in London.'

'Sounds like a great opportunity. A chance to make your mark on something, right from the very beginning.' Deep in the pit of Sophie's stomach, she was almost disappointed. If Drew had said that he was entirely at a loose end, then the chances of their paths crossing on a rather more permanent basis were greater.

'It is.' His chest heaved in a motion of regret. 'I'd rather it hadn't come my way in quite the way that it did.'

'Your hospital closing, you mean?'

'Yeah. I put everything into that place and when the local authority said it was to close, I fought as hard as I could. We had an action group, we lobbied everyone we could think of, got a local petition going.'

'It sounds as if you were very determined.'

'I was.' His fingers had been resting on the hand that she had looped through his arm, and suddenly he took them away. 'I didn't always have time for the people around me. My family and friends.'

Sophie caught her breath. He was warning her off. Telling her that he wasn't so different from her father. In one way that was a choking disappointment, but in another way… If he felt nothing for her, why would he even bother to say it?

'You have time tonight, though.'

They'd been walking more and more slowly, and suddenly he came to a halt. When Sophie faced him, standing right in his path, he took off his jacket and wrapped it around her shoulders in a gesture that screamed of gentle protectiveness.

'Tonight is… It's just tonight.'

'That's okay.' She wanted to shrug off his jacket and demand a more intimate warmth. The warmth of having his arms around her, right here, right now.

She knew he was tempted. But he shook his head. 'We shouldn't get carried away.'

'Do you mean *I* shouldn't get carried away. I've been doing some reading on the internet. Isn't there something about traumatic brain injury affecting your impulse control?'

'It can do. That's just one possible symptom.'

'Do you think that's the case here?'

His eyes searched her face. 'No. I don't.'

'Then maybe you're afraid that if you kiss me, I might forget all about it.'

One hand cupped the side of her jaw and she tilted her

face up towards his. So close. Then she felt his other arm around her waist, almost lifting her off her feet, pulling her against him. He kissed her, brushing his lips against hers as if he was feeling his way forward, gauging her reaction.

A little sigh escaped her lips. Couldn't he feel that she wanted more than that?

He kissed her again, properly this time. Deep and full of longing, offering himself up to her and taking what he wanted, all at the same time.

'You won't forget.' He almost growled the words, challenging her on the most primitive of levels.

'Do it again, then. Make sure…' She'd heard voices as people strolled past them in the darkness. Right now, she didn't care who recognised her or what they might say or do. All she cared about was Drew.

'Kiss me now, Taylor.'

His lips quirked into a smile. He knew that she was teasing him. 'That will be my pleasure…'

CHAPTER TEN

SINCE THE CRASH, waking up had been a slow process. Sophie had lost the ability to hit the ground running, knowing everything she had to do that day, remembering everything she'd done the day before. She took a breath, giving the memories time to come back and organise themselves in her head.

Opening one eye, she consulted the message written on her forearm in magic marker. Carly was with Mark at the hotel. She was at Drew's house, in his spare room. The door was open and the landing light was on. She must have asked him to do that last night so that she wouldn't wake in darkness and wonder where she was.

And he'd kissed her. She didn't need a note to herself to remind her about that. Even if a few of the delicious details had slipped her mind, her body remembered them. The way he'd kissed her until she'd been breathless. The way his lips had whispered everything that his body had said.

Big Ben had tolled midnight, the deep chimes echoing along the river. He'd tenderly let her go, and Sophie had reluctantly allowed him to. She hadn't run from him, leaving her glass slipper behind, but 'just for tonight' had meant what it said, all the same.

She rolled over, picking her phone up from the nightstand. She didn't remember putting it there, it should be in her bag. Sophie shrugged. Last night she'd done a lot of things to break her familiar routine.

The phone responded to her touch. Ten past nine. There was plenty of time before her appointment in Harley Street. She put the phone back onto the nightstand and lay back against the pillows.

Wait. That wasn't her phone… She stared at the corner of the instrument. It must be Drew's. He had the same model as her. But what was it doing in here? For the life of her, she couldn't remember him with it.

Doubt gnawed its way towards her heart. She didn't remember the photos that were on the internet being taken either. They'd been taken with a phone, too…

Drew wouldn't do that. He wouldn't. But trust and logic only went so far, and fear was a much more potent emotion. She sat up, reaching for the phone. She hated herself for finding the photo icon, in just the same place as it was on her own phone. It was wrong to tap it, and then scroll through the pictures.

A couple of photos of a woman, who resembled Drew, hugging a toddler. She remembered him saying he had a sister, who was married with a young child… She scrolled past them, and found a couple of pictures of his motorbike, and four of various bits and pieces that looked as if they came from an engine. Then nothing.

She was on a roll now. Somehow, relief didn't stop her from tapping to see whether he'd sent any texts or emails. Nothing. The last call listed was the one he'd made to book the restaurant yesterday. There was an incoming text…

Sophie couldn't help it. She opened the text. She vaguely remembered Carly and Drew talking about someone called Charlie, and supposed that was how Carly had got into contact with Drew in the first place.

You're in the papers again, mate.

Then she remembered. She and Drew had walked back to his car, and as he'd been helping her in she'd heard the sound of a shutter and been blinded for a moment by a bright flash. Drew had smiled, motioning the man with the camera away and shrugging the incident off.

Charlie obviously didn't think he'd be so indifferent to it. Maybe Drew was keeping score, the way that Josh probably had. How many times he could get himself in the papers, by dint of having Sophie on his arm.

A noise in the doorway made her jump. The phone slithered out of her hand and onto the floor.

'You're awake.' A faded pair of jeans, slung low on his hips, and a black T-shirt. Could he really have looked any more like the guy she should have had sex with last night?

He wasn't much of an actor, though. However much he wanted to pretend that he hadn't seen what she'd been doing, his body language said it all.

There was no point in trying to pretend that she hadn't been caught. He'd been caught as well. 'I seem to have ended up with your phone. You've got a text.' She got out of bed, recovering the phone from the floor, and held it out towards him.

'Yours is in the usual place, in your bag. I gave you mine last night so you could set an alarm for this morning.' He gave her the cup of coffee and inspected his phone. Shrugged and slipped it into his pocket.

That cleared up one unknown, but the other was still tearing at her. 'You saw the photographer last night…'

'Of course I saw him. I don't know how he caught up with us.'

'You didn't call him, then. Or this friend of yours…Charlie. It would have been a better shot if he'd got us…' She couldn't say *kissing.* She already felt as if the delicious audacity of that had been wrenched from her. '…on the Embankment.'

His face darkened. 'You think I *wanted* to be in the papers this morning?'

'Didn't you?'

'I'm a doctor, Sophie. I have a reputation to consider. I'm not some fly-by-night hanger-on, who thinks it's a good idea to wake up in the morning and read what he did last night.'

'Oh, so you think that I'm a fly-by-night do you?' He might have pretended to value what she did, but when it came down to it, his attitude was just the same as her father's.

'I didn't say that. If you want it in words of one syllable, then here it is. I'm not Josh.' He turned, pausing in the doorway. 'Get dressed. You have an appointment this morning.'

She'd never seen him so angry. He banged the door as he left, and Sophie heard his footsteps, marching along the hall and down the stairs.

Knives, forks. The butter dish, absolutely straight and in line with the marmalade. Drew arranged the breakfast table with ruthless accuracy, in an attempt to stop thinking about everything else.

The moment he'd seen her, sitting up in bed, looking at his phone, Drew had realised that she didn't trust him. And when she'd seen him, the look of guilty panic on her face had confirmed it.

Rationalise. He had to remember that Sophie had just woken up, and probably hadn't had a clue what his phone was doing beside her bed. She'd looked at it, and the text from Charlie had made it seem that he was just like Josh had been. How could she know that it was just the opposite, that he dreaded seeing his picture in the papers?

But she should have trusted him. She'd kissed him…

And that had been last night. They'd agreed that. Just one kiss, just one night.

Drew couldn't even bring himself to think about it. Of course it hadn't been *just* a kiss. He knew what just a kiss felt like, and it didn't leave his body aching for more, far into the night. Just a kiss would have felt uncomplicatedly good. Just a kiss didn't care if she didn't trust him.

A chair scraped as it was pulled back from the kitchen table, and Drew turned. She was wearing a pair of smart trousers with low pumps and a lacy sweater. Her hair pulled back in a ponytail, a couple of last night's curls escaping around her face. No one had any right to look this beautiful first thing in the morning.

'I want to apologise.' She looked at him determinedly, and all of Drew's anger melted. 'It was wrong of me to look at your phone, and your private texts, and it was wrong of me to suggest you had anything to do with the press finding us last night. I was being paranoid.'

'I was...' He shook his head. There was no excuse for his behaviour, other than the hurt of having those moments they'd had together twisted and warped by suspicion. 'You've every right to be concerned, after what you've been through. I should have understood that.'

He walked over to the table, pulling his phone from his pocket and putting it down in front of her. 'You can look at my phone any time you like. You can look through my laptop, through every drawer in this house. I promise you that you'll find nothing that compromises you.'

Her hand trembled as it hovered over the phone. Then she picked it up and handed it back to him. 'I don't need to, Drew. I know there's nothing.'

The impulse to kiss her was almost overwhelming. 'Are we good, then?'

She nodded, looking up at him with the smile that made him want her in the very worst of ways. 'Yeah. We're good.'

Drew had taken the hire car up to Harley Street this morning, loading their bags into the boot so that they could drive straight down to Devon after Sophie's appointment. As arranged, he drove into the narrow, paved mews which ran behind the impressive Georgian façade of Henry Chancellor's consulting rooms.

'Molly…?' His phone lay in the hands-free cradle on the dashboard.

'You're early.'

Drew grinned. Early was always a point in any patient's favour in Molly's book as it allowed her to run Dr Chancellor's diary with the minimum of fuss and the maximum of efficiency.

'It's the green door. I'm opening up now.'

A brightly painted garage door, one of the row that lined one side of the mews, began to move, sliding upwards to reveal a garage. Two cars inside and one free space. Drew turned into it and switched off the ignition, and the door closed behind them.

A switch, probably flipped from Molly's desk, and the light came on. Sophie turned to him, smiling.

'Very neat.'

He'd promised to get her inside the building without anyone seeing her, and had been gratified when she'd just nodded and taken him at his word, not demanding to know how he was going to manage it. Molly had come up trumps, allowing him to use the garage usually reserved for the doctors who worked in the building, and negating the need for Drew to roll Sophie up in a carpet and carry her up the front steps on his shoulder.

He got out of the car, squeezing through the gap he'd left between the driver's door and the wall, and opening Sophie's door as wide as the cramped space would allow.

'This way…' He led her up the steps to the door into the main building, and found Molly waiting there for them.

'Drew. How nice to see you.' Molly smiled at him, and then turned her attention quickly to Sophie. 'Welcome…'

It was the first time he'd ever heard Molly not address a patient by their name. Perhaps that was taking things a little too far, but after this morning the gesture was appreciated.

'Thank you.' Sophie was beginning to shake now, and Molly took her arm, leading her towards the back stairs.

'Dr Chancellor's the best in his field. Although he'd tell you that Drew is. A case of the pupil outstripping the teacher...'

'Drew's a bit of an upstart, then.' Sophie looked over her shoulder at Drew, giving him a tremulous smile.

'Definitely.' Molly laughed quietly. 'There are a few stories I could tell you...'

'Look after him.' Drew only just caught Sophie's whispered words and Molly's nod in response as they reached the top of the stairs. His heart almost burst. The one time when she should be worried for herself and she'd remembered him.

He walked through to the reception area at the front of the building and started to fiddle with the coffee machine next to Molly's desk. Sophie would be a while with Henry Chancellor, and suddenly each minute seemed to drag out in front of him like a potential eternity.

'No coffee...' Molly walked around her desk, bending to flip the switch of a socket on the wall, and the lights on the coffee machine went out.

'What?'

'I'll make you some herbal tea, Drew. I'm not having you sitting here drinking coffee and twitching like a cat on hot bricks.'

Drew sat down. This was Molly's waiting room, and he knew from experience that she ruled it with a rod of iron. Molly disappeared for a minute and returned with a cup and saucer, placing it firmly on the side table next to him.

'Drink that. Then you're going for a walk.' She pulled at the cuff of her smart blue jacket and glanced at a silver bracelet watch. 'Half an hour at least. You can pop down to Oxford Circus and do some shopping.'

'You want me to get something for you?'

'No, I want you out of here. Your friend will be fine, but Dr Chancellor needs to examine her and go through the results of the MRI scan. Then he'll be wanting to have a talk with her.'

Drew knew better than to argue with Molly. She was probably right anyway, she usually was. He shrugged, picked up his cup and sipped the tea.

When he arrived back at the consulting rooms, Molly was chatting to a young couple, taking their toddler onto her knee so she could play with the picture calendar on her desk. There was an agonising five-minute wait, and then Molly answered the phone, nodded into the receiver, and gave the child back to her mother. A glance in his direction indicated that Drew should follow her.

She led the way through to the back stairs, arriving just as Sophie appeared at the top of them. A warm smile in Sophie's direction, and then the two of them were bundled through the door that led to the garage, as Sophie stuttered out her thanks.

He shouldn't ask yet. He should let Sophie gather her thoughts and tell him in her own time. Drew opened the passenger door for her, squeezing around to the other side of the car and getting in. The garage doors opened, presumably under Molly's direction, and light filtered through into the gloom.

Drive. Just drive. Sophie was staring straight ahead of her, her face impassive. He knew that look, and she didn't need to have him question her at the moment. She was busy processing everything that had happened in the last hour. He put the car into reverse, cursing softly and jamming his foot on the brake as the sound of the front bumper touching the wall reached his ears.

That was all he needed. Rolling the car forward, he was about to try again when Sophie's voice sounded beside him.

'Steady… Everything's okay, Drew.'

His heart jumped. Okay how? Really okay? Drew was shaking now, and he took a deep breath before he turned towards her. He hadn't been prepared for this. The sudden realisation that Henry's assessment of the MRI scan results meant everything to him. That he needed to know, just as desperately as she did.

Then he heard her crying, softly. 'Soph…' Drew switched the engine off, turning to her. She was gulping for air now, her cheeks streaked with tears. 'Soph, it's all right. Whatever it is, we can face it.'

We can face it. It was no longer a matter of encouraging her, telling her that she was strong enough to deal with this. Drew realised that however hard he'd tried to stand back, however much he'd felt that was the best thing he could do for himself and for Sophie, that they were now in this together.

'It's…' She flung her arms around him, crying into his shoulder, her words coming between fits of tears. 'He said it was okay… The scan…'

It was as if his skin was suddenly porous, soaking up happiness. Drew felt it permeate through his body and he twisted in his seat, holding her tightly. 'It's okay. Just let it out, sweetheart…'

She clung to him for a long time. Finally she seemed to catch her breath and pulled away from him, her face shining. 'I want to get this right.' She pulled her notebook out of her bag.

'Take your time.' Drew grinned at her as she tore one of the pages, in her haste to get to the right place.

'Dr Chancellor said that the MRI scan showed up some microscopic lesions on the site of the impact…' She looked up at him, shrugging. 'Basically, I hit my head and that caused a mild traumatic brain injury. There's every reason to be optimistic about my symptoms improving and, of course, there are plenty of things I can do to manage the condition. There are no signs of any other bleeding or of any tumours.' She snapped her notebook closed triumphantly.

'Is that what you were worried about, Sophie?' Drew had never voiced his own concerns to her, knowing that they were not the most likely scenario, and that they would only feed her own fears.

She shrugged. 'I knew it wasn't likely. But anything's possible.'

'And now you know for sure.'

'Yes. Thank you, Drew. I wouldn't have had the scan or seen Dr Chancellor if you hadn't made me.'

'Did I make you? I thought it was just a little gentle encouragement.'

She snorted with laughter, reaching into her handbag for a tissue and blowing her nose. 'Were you going to let me get away with not going?'

'Now you mention it…' He grinned at her. 'I would have carried you here if you hadn't agreed to come. But that's not the point. You made that step yourself, and that means something.'

She nodded, her brow furrowing in thought. 'I'm ready now. I'm going to stop messing around and really work on coming to terms with this. Dr Chancellor's given me a whole list of things to do…' She reached into her bag and pulled out some sheets of paper, stapled together. 'He's given me a copy of the results and his recommendations, so I've no excuse for forgetting.'

Drew's fingers itched for the paper. He trusted Henry's judgement better than his own. Henry had been his guide and mentor since medical school. All the same, he wanted to see the results for himself, read them three times and check each word.

'I imagine he intended me to show them to you. I don't understand the medical bits.' She smiled at him. 'His recommendations were much the same as what you've been saying to me.'

The temptation to snatch the sheets from her fingers almost overwhelmed him. 'What do you say we find somewhere to have lunch and look at this? We'll go to Regent's Park, there must be a café there…'

'Okay.' She put the precious papers back into her bag, reaching for her seat belt and then changing her mind and letting it snap back into the housing. 'Thank you, Taylor.'

She planted a soft kiss on his cheek. Drew felt his skin tingle with pleasure where her lips had touched it. Then she grabbed the front of his shirt, pulling him as close as the restricted space would allow.

Her lips were so close her scent overwhelmed him. Drew meant only to brush his lips against hers, but that didn't work out. He found himself kissing her, his hand on the back of her neck, his thoughts racing in a dance of sheer delight. She responded to him so readily. So completely.

His phone beeped and he ignored it. Then, out of the corner of his eye, he caught sight of a tiny red light, flashing somewhere up by the roof of the garage.

'Soph… Sophie.' He let her go, feeling the loss immediately.

'What?' Her eyes sprang open, widening in confusion. 'I'm sorry…'

'Are you?' He grinned, running a finger along her jaw. 'I'm not. But perhaps this isn't the place…' He pointed to the CCTV camera mounted on the wall. He'd forgotten all about the screen on Molly's desk, where the feeds from the security system were displayed.

'Oops. We've been caught…' She put her hand to her mouth. Drew was tempted to get out of the car, tear the camera from its mounting and kiss her again. Instead, he reached for his phone.

A text from Molly.

Let me know when you've gone so I can close the garage doors.

Sophie looked over his shoulder and giggled.

'She's very tactful.'

'Yeah. Molly's the soul of discretion.'

She wound down the car window, waving to the CCTV camera with a smile and blowing a kiss. Drew's phone beeped again, and he showed Sophie the smiley face that Molly had sent. It was time for them to go. He started the car, backing carefully out of the cramped parking space in the garage.

CHAPTER ELEVEN

SOPHIE SEEMED TO be blooming. She had studied Henry Chancellor's recommendations carefully, and with Drew's help she was sticking to them. Her confidence seemed to grow by the day, and she became more relaxed and a delight to be with on set.

And then, unexpectedly, they both had a day off. This time it was Todd's scenes, not Sophie's, that needed to be reshot, and neither Drew nor Sophie were needed. He expected that she'd take the opportunity to have a lie-in and a lazy day.

Instead, she appeared at breakfast looking like a million dollars. A little make-up, skilfully applied to make it look as if she was bare-faced. A pretty top, swirls of green and blue, with a matching necklace.

'What are you up to today?' She plumped herself down opposite him.

'I've nothing planned.' Sophie clearly had, and whatever that was he suddenly craved the opportunity to be a part of it.

She grinned. 'In that case, can I persuade you to give me a lift? I need to go into town and then I'm going to visit the hospital.'

'What for?'

'I'm going to visit the children's ward. I made up my mind that I would when we were visiting Carly. I got lost on the way to the drinks machine and ended up in there.'

He chuckled. 'I thought you were just taking your time, so that I could persuade Carly to behave.'

'Nothing that premeditated. I phoned the administrator yesterday and he said it would be fine for me to go. I want to stop off in town to get something for them first. I can't go empty-handed.'

She didn't need to take anything, just being there would be more than enough. But he supposed a little memento of the afternoon for the kids would be nice.

'Sure. You want me to borrow a car? You might arrive a bit windblown if we take the bike.'

'Oh, windblown is fine.' She obviously had everything planned and was on a roll. 'I like the bike.'

He liked the bike, too. Particularly with Sophie riding behind him, her arms firmly around his waist. He took the longest route he could into town, hoping that it wasn't too obvious that he was just riding around with her for kicks.

'Phew!' She climbed off the back of the bike, removing her helmet and unzipping her jacket. 'I love those country lanes. There seem to be such a lot of them.'

She shot him a knowing grin, looked around and then made a beeline for the door of the large electrical store that he'd parked outside. The automatic doors swooshed open, and Drew followed in the wake of her bright enthusiasm.

Suddenly she stopped short, a frown puckering her brow. 'I didn't come in here for a vacuum cleaner, did I?' She was looking at the display straight in front of her.

'I wouldn't have thought so. You didn't say what it was you wanted.' Drew looked around for a clue.

She'd consulted her notebook and a grin spread across her face. 'Yeah, I think that would be good. What do you reckon?' She flipped the notebook around so that he could see what she'd written.

'A tablet computer. Yeah, that would be great to have on the ward. The kids can watch films, play games…'

'Good.' She looked around and then set off towards the far side of the shop. 'Come along.'

She listened to the salesman's spiel, tried out a few for herself, and then ignored his recommendation completely, choosing a model that Drew thought would be perfect. 'I'll take one. No, actually, I'll take two.'

'Yes, miss.'

Sophie leaned towards Drew, whispering in his ear. 'Do you think that's okay? I'm not having a problem with impulse control here, am I?'

'Maybe. You can afford it?'

She rolled her eyes. 'Of course I can.'

'And the kids will love these. When an impulse is as good as this one, who cares?'

She brightened. 'Yes… Of course. Who cares? What do you think about headphones? They might like headphones…' Her gaze searched the display behind the counter.

'It's a nice idea, but the hospital will want to have a different set for each patient. They probably already provide single use ones.'

'Good point. What about… If I get one of those gift cards, they can download some games and films.'

Drew nodded his approval. She was bright with enthusiasm, and totally irresistible along with it. 'It's a very generous gift. I imagine they'll be well used, a lot of hospitals are collecting money to buy these at the moment.'

'Hmm. Wonder if it was my idea or the admin guy's…' She shrugged. 'Doesn't really matter. As long as they like them.'

'No, it doesn't matter.' Drew suspected that she would have fretted over the point a few weeks ago, trying to remember something that wasn't there, and it was good to see her dismiss it with such carelessness.

'I thought about what you said. The other day. About believing in me.'

'Yeah?'

'I reckoned if someone like you could believe in me, then I'd give it a try.'

Drew caught his breath, humbled by her faith in him. 'And how's that going?'

'Not sure yet. Working on it.' She slipped her hand into the crook of his arm, watching while the salesman wrapped her purchases.

She made a point of taking the ward sister and the administrator to one side and handing them the bag containing the tablets privately. And Drew made a point of watching her do it. He enjoyed her delighted smile when the ward sister saw what was in the bag and thanked her.

He hung back, letting her work her magic. No fuss, no big entrances, she just chatted briefly to a couple of the nurses, then let the ward sister lead her to one of the beds, where a small girl was dwarfed by the medical equipment around her. Sophie was introduced to the woman by the bedside, who smiled, pulling up a chair for her, and she took the little girl's hand.

It was almost too much to bear. Drew thought that he'd seen just about everything that could happen in a hospital, both good things and bad. But this was an aspect of healing he hadn't seen before. She made sure that she went to each of the beds, taking a little joy with her as she did so. Talking to the staff and the families. Seeming to see only the kids, and not the paraphernalia that surrounded them. Playing with them, making faces, anything to make them smile.

And smile they did. Drew didn't blame them one bit. She was more beautiful than he could ever have imagined a woman could be, and if there had been a spare bed in the place, he'd have been tempted to get into it, just for that smile and the touch of her fingers on his.

Finally she found her way back to him. 'Sorry. I've been so long...'

He shook his head in astonishment. 'Don't. I love this.'

'Drew, there's this little boy. In the third bed along…'

'Yeah? What about him?'

'He loves motorbikes. He has a toy one, and I told him that I'd come on a motorbike…' Her expression was somewhere between imploring and embarrassed. 'I don't suppose you could…' She waved her hand vaguely at the window.

'Leave it with me. I'll be back.'

She brightened immediately. 'Thank you.'

Drew turned on his heel, grinning to himself.

He'd spoken to the ward sister and to Tommy's mother. It had been decided that, as the day was fine and warm, the young boy could be taken out into the grassy area outside the ward for a while. Drew went to fetch his bike from the car park, and rolled it as close as he could to the ward entrance, making sure that the stand held it firm and steady on the uneven ground.

Sophie had come outside with a little girl and one of the nurses, and the three of them were busy with the inevitable photographs. Drew sat down on a bench to wait, nodding at the burly man who was already sitting at the other end, drinking from a can.

'That's Sophie Warner.' The man nodded towards her knowingly.

'Yeah.' Drew wondered if the man saw what he saw, and came to the conclusion that he must do. It was impossible not to notice her smile.

'It's all very well, coming here, taking photographs. You'd think they wouldn't have the nerve.'

'It's nice for the kids. And the parents.' Drew wondered what planet the guy came from. Couldn't he see the pleasure that Sophie's visit was giving everyone?

'Then she'll go home and take a few more pictures. Put them up on the internet and then pretend she doesn't know how they got there.'

'And you're her best friend. Which is how you know all this.'

The man missed his sarcasm entirely. 'They all do it. Media whores, the lot of them. And from the sounds of it, she's the worst. I read what that bloke said in the paper, he seemed like a genuine type. Whore's the right word for her.'

The keys of his bike fell to the ground at his feet as Drew's hand balled involuntarily into a fist. 'Apologise.' He choked out the word. One last chance for the man before he punched him.

'Who to? Not you. And not *her* either.' The man got to his feet, throwing his half-empty can at a waste bin and missing it entirely. Drew stood, towering over the man, who realised he was outmatched and almost ran in the opposite direction from where Sophie was standing at the entrance to the ward.

The temptation to drag him back on his knees to apologise to Sophie almost overwhelmed Drew. Then he heard her laughter. Sophie was enjoying her day. He couldn't spoil it all for her, by letting her know that someone had called her a whore.

Every tendon ached for action of some sort. Punching something, kicking something—the inoffensive brick wall of the building seemed like a reasonable candidate at the moment. Instead, Drew bent, picked up his keys and slipped inside, making for the gents.

He filled a bowl with cold water, splashing his face and the back of his neck. Stared himself down in the mirror until he was able to breathe again. He had to calm down. If Sophie could deal with this, and still smile and face the world, then so must he.

Finally, he was calm enough to consider venturing out. He dried his face and hands and walked outside, making his way back to the ward. At the door, he ran headlong into Sophie's smile.

'There you are. Are you ready?'

'Yes, the bike's outside.'

'We're all set, too.' She grinned over to where Tommy had been seated in a wheelchair, beaming with happiness.

'Great. Let's do it.'

Tommy was wheeled out of the ward by a male nurse, his mother walking by his side. He was full of questions about the bike, and Drew bent down by the side of the wheelchair, giving the boy all the specifications, details of petrol consumption and how it ran on a long journey.

Then Drew helped Sophie into the saddle, and Tommy was wheeled in close beside her for the inevitable photographs. 'Can I sit on it?' Tommy's imploring voice was directed at his mother.

The question was passed along the line to the ward sister, who nodded a yes and supervised as Tommy was helped from his wheelchair and lifted onto the saddle in front of Sophie. She curled one arm protectively around his waist, and the male nurse stood behind them, supporting Tommy but looking for all the world as if he just wanted to be in on the photographs.

Drew approached Tommy's mother, who was waving at her son's delighted smile, tears streaming down her face. 'Why don't you go and stand with them? I'll take a picture.' He gestured at the phone in her hand.

'He doesn't want me…' The woman smiled up at him. 'When a guy's sitting on a bike with a film star, he generally doesn't want his mum around.'

'I can understand that.' It wasn't just Tommy who felt that way. 'But he'll have plenty of pictures with Sophie. Perhaps you'd like one to remember today by, too.'

She pressed her lips together. 'I look a mess.'

Drew smiled. 'You look fine.'

He held his hand out and she dropped her phone into his palm. Her hand flew to the elastic tie that held her hair back in a ponytail, and she produced a comb from her handbag, scraping it across her head.

The little group around the motorbike was about to break

up but Drew signalled to Sophie, who spoke quickly to the nurse who was holding Tommy, and they waited. A dash of lipstick, and Tommy's mother stepped forward. Sophie put her arm around her, pulling her a little closer so that she was in the centre of the frame with her son. When Tommy turned, beaming at his mother, Drew got the shot. Three more, for good measure, and then tears blurred his vision.

CHAPTER TWELVE

HUGGING HIM TIGHTLY all the way back to the hotel was the perfect ending to a perfect afternoon. Drew had seemed to take as much joy from it as she had and he'd talked about how much good it did the kids and their parents. Despite her father's clear disdain for the callow and useless profession his daughter had chosen, in Drew's eyes she was doing something important. Something that had brought him to tears at one point. He'd wiped them away quickly, but she'd seen them.

'Everyone looks busy.' He'd waited for her to get off the back of the bike and was surveying the scene of activity in front of the hotel.

'Looks as if Joel's happy with the scenes they shot today. We might be on the move.' Sophie had tried not to think about the impending move. A new set of hotel corridors to get lost in. Pages of notes that needed to be made, just so she could present some semblance of normality to the world around her.

He pulled one of his gloves off and his hand wandered to her arm, as if he was steadying her. As if he knew that she was standing on the edge of a dark precipice and that all she could do was jump, along with the others, and hope that everything was going to be okay.

'I thought we weren't moving to Hertfordshire until the

weekend.' He swung off the seat of the motorbike, unzipping his jacket.

'We've been making good time. If everything went well today, then there's only another day's filming before we're ready to go.'

'In that case…' he started to stroll towards the entrance of the hotel and Sophie followed him '…there's something I've been meaning to discuss with you.'

'What's that?'

'This might be a good time to think about restructuring things so they work a bit better for you.'

'You mean, facing the facts instead of hiding from them?'

'I wouldn't put it in those words exactly.'

She grinned up at him. 'Stop being nice to me, Drew. It unnerves me. And you know I get confused when you don't say exactly what you mean.'

He chuckled, taking her key along with his own from the receptionist. 'Okay, then. Now you've finally decided that being a diva isn't going to solve your problems, it's about time you looked squarely at your other options.'

'That's better.' She grinned up at him. 'So what *are* my other options?'

'Staying somewhere away from the crew, where you can get some peace and quiet…' He counted on his fingers. 'Having a therapist with you for all or part of the day. Telling Joel…'

She took the key to her suite from his hand and opened the door. 'Telling Joel. Are you sure about that one?'

'No. It's just a suggestion. You know your own business better than I do, and you can assess the possible implications, but I think that Joel knowing could help you with the day-to-day things.'

Sophie sat down with a bump.

Everything he'd said was perfectly reasonable. It would all help her cope on her own. That wasn't what was tearing at her.

'What about you, Drew?'

His gaze became solemn. 'What about me?'

'Are you…thinking about leaving?' Sophie felt a lump rise in her throat.

'It's a possibility. I'm going to have to at some point. I've got a job to go to, and you're going back to the States when filming's finished here.'

And that was set in stone. No way out for either of them, unless… No. It was too big a step to take. She couldn't see everything she'd worked for crumble, just for the sake of a man, not even Drew. She just didn't have the ability to trust that much any more.

'You're saying that I don't need you around any more?'

'That's up to you to decide.' Something in his eyes told her that her decision was important to him.

'Okay. You're right. I don't actually need you. Henry Chancellor could suggest a good memory therapist, couldn't he?'

'Yes. He'd do that.'

She looked into his face. Saw the tightening of his jaw and the slight beat of a pulse at his temple, which answered the biggest question of all.

'I don't *need* you, Drew. But if you feel able to, I really *want* you to stay.'

His smile was all the answer she needed. 'Yeah. I want to stay.'

'Life on set's not so bad, then?' He didn't seem to bristle with disapproval now, the way he had when he'd first arrived.

'I'm getting to like it.' He grinned. 'It's not what I thought it would be.'

'Is that settled, then?'

'Yeah. It's settled. There's another thing I was thinking of asking you.'

'Go on. We may as well get it all over with in one go.'

Sophie was almost breathless with relief. There was nothing which could hurt her now.

'We're going to be in London and my place is forty-five minutes' drive from the set. If you wanted, you could come and stay with me. You'd have a chance to settle a bit. Not so difficult to find your way around…' He shrugged, as if that probably wasn't an option at all.

'Are you sure? You might find the paparazzi on your doorstep. That wouldn't do your career much good.'

A slight flicker, at the side of his eye, attested to the fact that it had occurred to him, but it seemed that Drew was dealing with it. 'I want you to stay, Sophie.'

'In that case, I guess I don't have much choice.'

It was all settled. After some thought and a great deal of discussion, Drew called Joel, who appeared at the door of her suite inside two minutes.

'Sophie. You want to talk?'

'I do…' Drew took the initiative, seating everyone comfortably, keeping the atmosphere friendly and relaxed. He explained Sophie's condition clearly, the way he'd already discussed with her, emphasising the ways forward now that she'd been diagnosed and could get proper treatment.

'This is… There's no cure for this?' Joel rubbed his forehead thoughtfully.

'Time is the cure.' Drew smiled. 'Sophie's already made enormous improvements, working on her own. With a proper support framework, she can do everything she used to.'

Joel nodded. 'I was looking at some of the footage last night. The scene in the tea shop.'

'Yes?' Sophie gulped out the word. Joel was going to tell her that he wanted to reshoot. That was going to mean expense and inconvenience for everyone.

'It's fantastic, Sophie. There's a real depth to your performance, you've caught all the underlying sadness of the situation perfectly.'

'Thank you.' She didn't quite believe it, but Joel didn't lie about this kind of thing. That was what made him so good at his job.

'I wish you'd come to me with this sooner.'

So did she. It was the one thing she had no answer for, but Drew was there with one.

'You have to understand how difficult it's been for Sophie. Brain trauma isn't like a cut or a bruise. There's a long sequence of coming to terms with it, trying to understand what's happened.'

Yes. That was it. Sophie waited for Joel's response, her mouth dry.

'I'm glad you've talked to me now, then. Whatever you need, I want to hear about it.'

'Yes.' Sophie nodded. 'Thank you.'

'There is one thing,' Drew cut in smoothly. 'We've already agreed that this conversation remains between the three of us. I just want to reiterate it.'

'I hear you. But releasing this to the press, carefully and in the proper way, might get them off your back a bit, Sophie. It might give you a bit of leverage with regard to those photographs that got leaked onto the internet. If you weren't well when they were taken, that has to be grounds to suppress them.'

Drew's gaze flipped to her face. She could almost see him putting two and two together. Sophie had never quite been able to fathom whether Drew knew about the pictures or not, but now it was pretty clear. He hadn't known and now he did.

She wanted the earth to open up and swallow her. Or maybe it would be better if it swallowed Joel, before she decided to strangle him.

'Anything to do with the press is Sophie's decision. Not yours or mine.' Drew had regained his composure quickly, and was talking now to Joel. 'It's very important that Sophie's the one in control here. It's her memory that is impaired, not her understanding or her decision-making process.'

Right. In control. Whatever had made her think that was even possible.

'Okay. Understood.' Joel made a zipping motion across his mouth. His own, familiar way of confirming that his lips were sealed. That was all a bit late now.

'Is there anything else?'

'No…' Drew leaned back in his chair in an unconvincing parody of relaxation. 'Although we might get back to you with something.'

'Make sure you do.' Joel nodded to Drew, smiled at Sophie and got to his feet.

After Joel left, they were silent for long minutes. Drew was the first to break.

'Josh took compromising pictures, didn't he? Then he leaked them onto the internet, out of spite.'

'Spite and money. All of the gossip about the photographs didn't do him any harm when it came to selling his story. He's got a reality show on the back of it. I suppose he'll have a few things to say about me then.'

Just when she should have been elated, full of the success of finally getting things under control and being able to talk to Joel, she was suddenly beaten again. It was almost too cruel to bear.

'That's just sick. Can't you get them taken down?'

'Not legally. My lawyer tried, but they're Josh's copyright. His story is that I leaked them, for the publicity. Maybe I did… I don't remember.'

'I haven't seen them, Sophie. I won't be looking for them either.'

'Thank you.' She hung her head so he couldn't see her tears.

'If you ever want to talk about it, you know I'm here for you. But since you obviously don't…'

'I'm so ashamed, Drew.' She blurted out the words. For

once he didn't seem to know what to do. He reached forward to touch her, and ended up grazing his fingertips against her sleeve.

'Don't be.' He was thinking before he spoke, long gaps of silence between each sentence. 'You have nothing...nothing to be ashamed of. And you don't have to explain anything to anyone, least of all me. I know you didn't leak those photographs because I know you.'

They sat in silence. A minute and then two. Five and then ten. It was as if the photographs could be somehow wiped away if they didn't talk about them.

'Soph.' He finally spoke.

'Yes, Drew.'

'Do you want to get some ice cream?'

Somehow ice cream was the only thing that made sense. 'I'll call down to room service.'

'Or I was thinking maybe we could go into town for it.'

A twenty-mile round trip to get ice cream. That made sense as well, in a crazy kind of way.

'We'll go on the bike?'

'Yeah. I'd like that.'

'Good. Ice cream, then.'

The bike was always the place where Drew worked out his problems. Perhaps it could work the same magic for Sophie. She had to cling to him, her arms tight around his waist, and he sensed that the enforced proximity was as comforting to her as it was to him. Closeness that held no unwanted implications and none of the awkwardness that a hug might have engendered.

How could he not have known? Her agonised insistence that she had to retrieve the memories of those lost days. The morning he'd found her going through his phone. The idiot at the hospital. It was if he hadn't wanted to know.

Maybe he hadn't. Maybe he'd been afraid of what the photographs might show him. Gina's photographs had shown him much, much more than he'd ever wanted to know.

A slight change in the angle of the bike, reflected by a synchronous moment in their bodies, his and hers. He couldn't imagine the agony that Sophie must be in. Not being able to remember how something like that had happened. The constant questions, none of which had any answers.

Her hand moved, tapping his right side. She wanted him to go right at the next junction. It would take them on a huge detour along miles of country roads, which finally curved back on themselves and meandered into the high street. Drew smiled, turning the bike. Somehow, he and Sophie would get through this.

CHAPTER THIRTEEN

DREW WAS FEELING pretty pleased with himself. He'd succeeded in what he'd gone out to do and that always pleased him. They'd made the trip to London by train the previous evening, leaving his bike packed securely on one of the lorries that travelled with the crew and Jennie in charge of Sophie's luggage. Sophie had gone upstairs to unpack her overnight bag, returned to sit with him for half an hour and had then started to yawn so had gone straight to bed.

This morning she was fresh, rested and already settling in. By the time Drew was finished in the shower, she'd made breakfast, and then she'd sat down with her script, studying her lines for that afternoon. He'd pushed back the chairs in the sitting-room and she'd read them out loud, over-acting for laughs. She was spreading her wings, gaining in confidence and learning to do all the little things she'd once depended on him for. Soon she'd fly away.

Not today, though. The cast was meeting on set at one to take a look around and go through a few scenes. Inhabiting the place, Joel called it. Sophie was eager to get going, and by twelve they were already on the road.

'Stop here, will you? I think we need to take a turn soon.' She was studying the map on her phone intently.

'No, it's not for another few miles.' Drew stopped the car even so, and leaned over to peer at the screen in front of her. 'We're here.'

'Right under the blue dot. Yeah, I got that.' She smirked at him.

'And you need to scroll up a bit to get to where we're going. The Hazlemere Estate.'

'There's somewhere I want to stop off. It won't take long.'

'But rehearsals…'

'They're at three o'clock. I lied.'

'You lied? You need a good memory to be a good liar, don't you?' Sophie was up to something. He just couldn't fathom what.

'I wrote it down.' She picked her notebook up from her lap, flipping it open and displaying a page.

Rehearsals at three.
Tell Drew to leave at twelve.
Belltower Hospital.

'No. Not a chance, Sophie.'

She turned to him, the slow burn of her mismatched eyes boring through his defences. Maybe he'd have to give up trying to fight her on this one and just beg.

'I've heard an awful lot about my needs. What's best for me. And I'm sick of it. What about the things you need?'

'I don't need to go back to the hospital. It's closed. Finished.'

'Did you say goodbye?'

He'd been too busy to say goodbye. Writing references for the people who'd worked for him, arranging transfers of patients, speaking to the doctors at the new hospital to ensure that no one fell through the cracks of the bureaucratic process. He'd simply gone home one night, so tired that he could hardly stand, and had woken up the next morning with nowhere to go.

'Since you're not answering, I have to assume that's a no.'

'I didn't need to. It's done. Over.'

'Humour me.'

If he was humouring her, it wouldn't hurt so badly. If he thought that Sophie needed to go to the hospital for some reason, he'd bundle away his own feelings and go. 'You really think I should go?'

'Yes, I do.'

Wordlessly, he started the engine. There was only one person who could have made him go back and say the goodbyes he'd shrunk from before. And he had the misfortune to be in a car with her and heading towards the hospital entrance.

It was Sophie's face, not his own, that got them past the security guard at the entrance. That was almost the hardest thing to take.

'How did you do that?' He accelerated past the wooden hoardings.

'Jennie found out who to call for me. Then I got on the phone and said I was looking for a location.' She grinned. 'Sometimes having a well-known name works.'

'A location for what?'

'I didn't say. I said it was top secret and that probably nothing would come of it. Park over there.'

Drew swung the car into the ambulance bay in front of A and E. It seemed strange to be able to park here without causing an obstruction, but he imagined that the entrance to the pay-and-display car park would be chained shut. He got out of the car, stretching his legs and back.

'We can go in here, I think.' She handed him the keys that the security guard had given her and Drew sorted through them to find the right one. His hand shaking, he unlocked the door.

Sophie slipped her hand into his and Drew stepped inside. The smell of disinfectant had given way to a slight musty smell, and there was a layer of dust on the long, curved reception desk. Beyond, the cubicles had been denuded of their curtains, and all of the medical supplies and equipment had been removed, probably to be used somewhere else.

'It's so quiet.' Sophie was looking around, seeming to be trying to take in every detail of the place.

'Yeah.' There was nothing here. Nothing that he remembered, only bricks and mortar. 'Would you like to see my department?'

'Yes.'

Neurology was the same. Drew's old office was quiet and dusty, the room completely cleared apart from his desk and a couple of chairs. He flipped open his desk drawer, realising that he'd never thought to empty it before he'd left, and felt a stab of indignation when he found that someone else must have done it for him. Vaguely he wondered where his mug had got to. Broken and put into a rubbish bag, to be carted away, he supposed.

'This must be yours.' Sophie appeared in the doorway, holding his racing green and gold 1936 Grand Prix winner's mug between her thumb and forefinger. 'I tried to wash it but there's no water in the taps.'

'Where did you find it?' Drew took the mug from her, inspecting the mould culture that was growing inside.

'In the cupboard over the sink in the main office. Someone must have stuck a load of them in there without washing them.'

'Hmm. I'll take it home with me.'

Sophie produced a plastic carrier from her handbag and handed it to him, sitting down in the visitor's chair on the other side of his desk. 'This is where it all happened, then?'

Drew dusted off his chair, and sat, facing her. 'Yeah. All of it.'

'When I think of what that hour in Dr Chancellor's office meant to me…' She gave a little shrug. 'All the patients you saw here, each one of them must remember this office, and what you did for them.'

'Sometimes I wasn't able to give them good news…'

'No, I imagine not. But I know you still helped them.'

'I did my best.' It felt as if the most important part of his life had been lived in this place. The work he'd done. The people he'd worked with.

'You wrote your academic papers here? In the dead of night when everyone had gone home?' Her lips twitched into a smile in response to Drew's surprised glance. 'I saw them in the bookcase in your sitting-room.'

'Yeah, I spent a few nights here. Drank quite a bit of coffee.'

'And you feel you've left all that behind?'

Drew looked around the bare office. 'It's not here any more.'

'No, it's not. That's because you already took it with you. All you left behind was bricks and mortar. And your coffee mug.'

Something fell into place. When he'd left here he'd felt numb, not able to comprehend that it was all over. Now he realised that it wasn't.

'I worked so hard to keep this place open. When it closed, I felt that everything I'd done here was a failure, wiped out somehow. But it's not, it never was.'

She smiled. 'No. I used to hate moving from place to place when I was filming, but I learned that you take the good things with you. Which is why you have to do as many good things as you can, so you've got plenty to take when you go on to the next place.'

He smiled. 'That's a very nice thought. So I'll be taking lots of you with me, then. All the good things you've done for me.'

'Have I?' She seemed genuinely surprised. 'I thought I'd just be taking lots of you.'

'Let's not think about that now.' One parting at a time. However much she'd eased the pain of this one.

'No. Best not.'

He reached for her hand, curling his fingers around hers. 'I'm glad we came, but I think it's time to go now.'

'On to the next place?'

'Yeah.' He smiled at her. 'On to the next place.'

He felt somehow lighter when he got back into his car. Sophie returned the keys to the guard with a smile and a thank you, and he opened the gate, letting them out. He would never have come here again without Sophie, and this time he was leaving well. Moving on, instead of crawling away, paralysed by failure and regret.

The Hazlemere Estate was another fifteen minutes drive. A three-lane motorway gave way to leafy country lanes, and when he turned into the gates Drew saw one of the set security guys, waving him through and along a long gravel drive.

He hadn't known this house was even here. Buried in the countryside, behind wrought-iron gates and surrounded by trees at the perimeter of the estate. It was a hidden gem, its architecture spanning a hundred years from Georgian to Victorian as successive generations had added to the country pile that they'd inherited. And now it seemed to have slipped back in time, and sat in the sunshine of an afternoon some time in 1944.

Drew took a long look at the vintage car parked outside and wondered if it was driveable. One of the set mechanics strolled over to look at his own car.

'This is yours?'

Drew nodded. 'I restored her myself.'

'Nice. Shame she's not a little bit older, we could have used her.'

'Betty would like that.' Sophie got out of the car and joined them.

'Betty?' Both men turned to Sophie at the same time, and Drew raised an eyebrow. Not only had Sophie taken the radical step of naming his car, but it seemed that she remembered what she'd called it.

Sophie shrugged. 'She seems like a Betty to me. A bit old-fashioned, but kind of sleek and beautiful.'

The mechanic shot Drew a look that suggested that somehow Sophie didn't understand the lure of engine oil and grease, and asked Drew if he could take a look at the engine. Drew passed his car keys over and they were pocketed carefully.

'So this is the hospital?' He looked up at the impressive façade in front of them.

'Yes. Apparently a lot of country houses were converted into hospitals during the war.' She gave the information with a hint of relish and Drew smiled. Three weeks ago she would have probably kept her mouth shut, feigning disdain, but now she was willing to risk being interested.

'Shall we go in?'

The massive wooden front doors were open, and inside the place was a different world. A huge hallway, which had been converted into a reception area, in nineteen-forties style. Right in front of them stood a carved wooden desk, with a visitors' book, paper and a fountain pen.

Sophie picked the pen up, examining it, and then put it back in place. They followed the signs and found themselves in a large room, complete with fireplaces and chandeliers, that contained rows of beds, placed close enough together to give a modern staff nurse a seizure.

'Amazing.' Drew looked around him. There was nothing which could possibly be traced back to the last seventy years here. It was just as if a snapshot had been taken of the house's chequered history, and re-created perfectly.

'Yes. This is very good.' Sophie was studying the space carefully, and he knew that she was running through her own lines in her head, putting them in the context of their surroundings.

Suddenly, Dr Tara Green surfaced. Sophie even walked slight differently, her own personality subsumed by that of the serious, yet unworldly Dr Green. She moved around the space, looking at everything, testing the height of the beds with her hand, trying random lines from the script under her breath.

Then she was back again. 'How do you do that?' Drew grinned at her.

Sophie shrugged. 'It's about getting yourself into the mindset. People think that learning lines is the only thing an actor has to remember. It's a lot more than that.'

He was beginning to see that. And the more he saw, the more he understood Sophie's achievement. Keeping going, telling no one. 'It must have been very hard for you, Soph.'

She nodded, her face suddenly pinched with stress. 'Yes. It's better now.' She brushed the thought away, smiling again as she looked around the room. 'You need a good memory for make-believe.'

It was just make-believe, all of it. But it was underpinned by serious work and research, not the useless, brittle dreams he'd first thought it was. Drew could respect that.

They explored some more, popping their heads around doors to find rooms that remained untouched and were part of a modern family home, albeit rather grand, next door to rooms that were part of a different time and space.

'Are you going to get some tea? While we rehearse?' The corridors were filling up now, familiar faces greeting them, and Joel's voice sounded, booming from the main hallway.

'I'll watch if that's okay.'

'You can go. I won't fluff my lines.' She seemed unaccountably reluctant to have him on set this afternoon.

'Nah. I'll watch.'

The actors spent some time walking around, discussing with Joel how they wanted to use the space. Drew was becoming used to the process. Reading through the script. Talking about how the words would work in the three-dimensional context of the set. Then a run-through of the scene that Sophie had been learning that morning.

It was different this time. As she and Todd worked together, the lines he'd heard took on emotion and a subtle depth of meaning that he'd missed the first time around. Between them the tension started to build, and even though neither was in costume, the spell they wove was so complete that Drew forgot that what they were saying wasn't real.

Drugs had been stolen from the medicine cabinet. Sophie accused one of Todd's men and he responded with denials. The argument that raged between them mounted in intensity, the atmosphere made all the more compelling by the fact that they kept their voices low, as if afraid someone would hear them. Joel was nodding, letting the scene play through in its entirety, allowing the actors their heads.

Then the climax. Todd pulled Sophie against him, and she struggled. Instinctively, Drew almost propelled himself forward, ready to extract her from his grasp, and then she melted into his arms. The words that Drew had imagined would have been spoken as a curt acceptance of his story fell from her lips in a husky whisper. Then she kissed him.

Drew's hands fisted at his sides. He knew what was in the script. But somehow his mind had skirted around the kiss, imagining only a chaste peck on the cheek. This was nothing like that. She was standing on her toes, her fingers caressing his neck. And his hand was sliding slowly down her back.

'Steady, tiger. They're pretending.' A quiet whisper in his ear jolted him back to reality and he looked round to see Jennie standing beside him.

'Yeah. Powerful scene,' he whispered back, so as not to break the silence, and Jennie nodded, seemingly mollified.

When he looked back at them they were *still* kissing. Dammit, this was a rehearsal wasn't it? Couldn't Todd save those moves until the cameras were rolling? Then Sophie pulled away from him, flattening herself against the wall, and raised her arm. The slap was pulled at the last moment, and her fingers hardly touched Todd's face, but his head rolled as if he'd taken full force of the blow. He caught her wrist in his hand, stopping her from delivering a second.

Oh, for crying out loud! Really? He kissed her again, with savage intensity, and she responded, whimpering with what Drew fondly supposed was a fake reaction. Then Todd turned, storming from the room, leaving Sophie leaning against the wall, her fingers over her lips as if something had just happened and she was wondering quite what it was.

'Great. Do that again tomorrow.' Joel's voice broke the silence.

Sophie and Todd exchanged a nod and a smile, and a buzz of conversation filled the set. Drew silently slipped away. Perhaps it *would* have been better to spend his time in one of the chairs that surrounded the catering truck, reading a book and drinking tea.

CHAPTER FOURTEEN

HALF AN HOUR LATER, she found him doing just that. Or, in truth, pretending to do just that. The tea tasted foul, and he hadn't read a word on the page in front of him. He forced a smile when she asked him if he was ready to go, and, not trusting himself to talk to her, resorted to the pretence that the busy roads required his full attention all the way home.

She followed him through into the kitchen. 'What?'

He'd just been shown his place, that was what. He'd told Sophie that a relationship between them was a bad idea, they'd talked about partings, and she'd taken him at his word. All Drew could think about was the way she'd kissed Todd.

He turned, manufacturing a smile. 'Nothing. I'm just tired.' He reached for the cups in the cupboard, putting the kettle on to give himself something to do. 'Are you hungry?'

'Not really. Upset's a better word for it.' She was eyeing him steadily.

'There's no reason—'

'It's just acting, you know. That's what I am. An actress.'

'You don't have to explain yourself to me, Sophie.'

'Right. Which is why you're sulking, is it? It seems that I *do* have to explain myself.' She sat herself down at the kitchen table, rubbing her face with her hands.

'You're just tired, Sophie.' The words slipped out before he had a chance to stop them. *Way to go. Blame her condition for your own hang-ups.*

She shot him a look that would have probably sliced the kitchen table in half, had it not been directed straight at him. 'That's your excuse, is it? Poor little Sophie's tired? Grow up…Taylor.'

'Forgotten my name again?' It was a cruel taunt, and he should have known better. Sophie's confidence was fragile…

'Is that all you can say? Yeah, okay, I get angry and I forget things. Big deal.' She jutted her chin confrontationally. 'Now who's being a diva?'

'What exactly are you accusing me of, Sophie?'

'This is supposed to be a friendship, you're not my doctor. It's not all a matter of me spilling my guts and you listening. And you can't pass your own moods off as me being tired.'

He wondered whether she was going to walk away from him, and realised that was just what he wanted right now. Sophie would walk away, shut herself in the spare room for a while and the matter would be closed. That would have suited him just fine.

'Well…?' Sophie jabbed the table with her finger. Clearly she was going nowhere.

'It just…it pushed a few buttons. It's nothing to do with you.'

'Only you made it to do with me, didn't you?'

He supposed he had. Drew sat down at the kitchen table, opposite her. 'It was a long time ago, Soph.'

'And…?' She wasn't letting him off the hook. Somewhere, deep inside, he was glad of it. This new Sophie, the one who was more than a match for him, was much more tricky to deal with, and infinitely more alluring.

'It's a stupid thing…'

'They usually are. Go on.'

Drew sighed, and gave up. 'I had a girlfriend. Years ago. She was beautiful, long dark hair, bright blue eyes…'

'I hate her already. So what did this lustrous-eyed temptress do, then?'

'Gina worked in local government but all she could think about was being a model.'

'Fair enough. Sounds better than local government any day.' Sophie's tone had softened. She knew she'd won, and she was tender in her victory.

'Yeah. I encouraged her, it was what she wanted. She got a few minor jobs, and loved it. Landed a bigger contract and gave up her day job.'

'Okay. Risky, but I can't talk. I took a few risks myself when I was starting out.'

'She didn't show me the pictures. The first I saw of them were a couple of nurses laughing over them in the canteen.'

Sophie gave a pained look, as if she knew just what was coming. 'Were they any good?'

'They were fabulous. She looked like a million dollars. She was posing with this guy, and he was…' Drew tried to put it delicately. 'Let's just say that if he hadn't had his hands strategically placed…'

'Okay. I get it.' Sophie took a deep breath. 'You do know, don't you, that what the camera sees really isn't what's going on. Models, actors, we all work pretty hard to construct something imaginary.'

'The camera always lies?' Drew still wasn't quite convinced of that.

'No, not always. But a professional model's job is not to show the truth. It's to sell a fantasy.'

'I…I don't know about that. I tried to talk to Gina about it, and she wouldn't…'

'Maybe it was something she was trying to get to grips with. We all have to.' Sophie shrugged. 'I'm trying to give her the benefit of the doubt here. Even if I'm not sure I want to.'

'I know. You don't need to be that generous, Soph. I know what happened. She got lost in it all, spent more and more time away from home, and I resented it. There were rumours about what was happening and…in the end she didn't deny them and we split up.'

She nodded, pressing her lips together. 'Personal relationships are tough in this business.'

'In my business too. I went to pieces over it. Henry Chancellor was my professional mentor at the time, and he called me in and hauled me over the coals. Told me that I could let everything slide, or I could work it out of my system.'

'And you worked?'

'Yeah. I've never let a relationship get in the way of my work since.' Drew turned the corners of his mouth down. 'As a number of my ex-girlfriends will tell you.'

'I'll take your word for it. I'd rather not take up references.'

Despite himself, Drew smiled. Sophie had a way of making almost anything seem possible. 'I'm sorry, Soph. It's about my own hang-ups and nothing you've done. You understand that, don't you?'

'Yeah. And tonight's not the time to argue.'

'No. I'm not sure any time is.' Suddenly Drew was trapped, between the enticing thought of what he wanted tonight to be for and the sure knowledge that the idea was impossibly reckless.

'Tonight…' She seemed to be pondering the options. Drew was wondering whether he ought to offer her a cup of tea when she rose, her movements slow and purposeful. Pulled the elastic tie from her hair and shook her head. Drew felt himself falling.

She leaned towards him, palms flat on the tabletop. Then one knee. Slowly, like a beautiful tiger, stalking its prey. He was caught motionless in her gaze. 'Soph…?'

Her lips brushed his. So soft. So sweet. And then he was on his feet, lifting her across the barrier between them, holding her tight against him. He felt her legs, curling around his hips, the high heels of her boots against the backs of his thighs, and he settled her weight against him. They fitted together like the last two pieces of a jigsaw puzzle.

She kissed him again. Annihilating his sense of anything other than her lips, her body.

'That's real. You get the difference?'

'I get it.'

He felt her smile against his lips. 'Come to your senses then, Taylor?'

Not even close. If his senses hadn't been scattered like broken glass on the floor, he wouldn't be doing this. Wouldn't be loving it, far more than he had any right to.

'This is not a good idea, Sophie.' Still he couldn't bring himself to let her go. 'You're going back to the States, I have a job here...'

'I know. Not tonight, though.' She moved against him in a way designed to arouse, and got exactly what she wanted.

'You're not making this easy, Soph...'

'You want me to?'

'No.' He kissed her again, meaning to make it into a regretful parting, and found himself taking every last drop of pleasure from it, then going back for more. 'Are you sure, Sophie?'

He needed more than just the messages her body were giving. He needed her to say it, so there was no mistake. Without that certainty, he would find a way to tear himself away from her.

She looked up at him. Clear-eyed and meltingly beautiful. 'I understand exactly what we're doing. I won't forget.'

She wriggled out of his grip, her feet finding the floor. When she reached for her bag, Drew thought she was going for her notebook, and smiled to himself. Maybe not the most romantic of gestures, but in this context it was everything.

Turning her back on him, she nestled against him. It was sweet agony. She pulled his arm around her, pulling up the sleeve of his shirt. Then he felt the tip of her magic marker against his skin.

'Sophie…' He kissed the top of her head, and then bent to kiss her neck, pushing the bright strands of hair out of the way. Even the touch of the pen on his forearm was making the small hairs stand on end.

'Is that clear enough?'

He looked, and saw the words. *Yes. Everything. Just for tonight.*

'It's clear.' He turned her around, taking the pen from her and pulling her into his arms. She clung to him, laughing with delight as he lifted her, bending forward to lay her down on the tabletop. Her breathing quickened, and he wondered if she thought he was going to take her right here.

Not a chance. If this was just for tonight, it would happen well, not in a haze of rushed passion. He stretched her arm over her head, tugging at her sleeve, and pulled the cap from the pen with his teeth.

'Now you.'

'What are you going to do?' She wriggled beneath him, and he pinned her down with the weight of his body.

'Stay still. Just a little *aide-memoire…*'

She'd been dozing in the soft warmth of his arms, and it was beginning to get dark when she opened her eyes. Drew greeted her with a lazy smile. 'Hey, there.'

Sophie looked around the room. His bedroom, she supposed, since it wasn't the spare room that she'd spent the night in last night. 'Hey. Who are you again?'

For a moment panic bloomed in his eyes, and then he relaxed into a smile. 'Don't do that to me.'

She kissed him, stretching her body luxuriantly against his. 'I thought you might give me a rerun. Just to freshen up on the details.'

Mischief tugged at the corners of his mouth. 'Where do you want me to start?'

'I remember this.' She held out her arm. He'd kissed her, writing his pledge for the night and drawing little hearts and flowers around it, with shooting stars running around her elbow. 'Does this last until morning?'

'It does. Once it's in writing, it's a done deal. You remember what happened next?'

'You carried me upstairs and took my clothes off. Then yours, and we kissed a bit.' She leaned in close to whisper in his ear. 'That was nice.' She ran her finger over his lips in a broad hint that he might repeat the exercise.

'So we did.' Drew kissed her. Without the hard edge of uncertain hunger this time. Now he knew what they could do together, knew exactly what response he could tease out of her.

She was more confident, too. She knew how he wanted her to touch him, how a soft stroke made him shiver deliciously, and a harder one made him groan out loud. The circle of cause and effect began to spiral between them again.

'You remember this?' He rolled on his back, pulling her shaking body on top of him, astride his hips. 'I wanted to feel your rhythm…'

He'd been inside her then. This time they mimicked the act, staring into each other's eyes. Stretching each moment to breaking point, luxuriating in the sweet fusion of past and present.

'When you came…' he stretched one arm up to brush his fingers against her lips '…you came so hard, I swear I could feel it.'

The memory of it pulsed through her body, making her shiver. 'You liked that?'

'I loved it. Then you called out my name…'

'Tay—lor…' Sophie bent to kiss him, wondering if he minded. 'You were blowing my brains out, Drew. I couldn't think…'

He grinned. 'If you had called me anything else, I'd have reckoned I needed to try a bit harder.'

'You didn't need to try any harder. If you had I probably would have passed out.'

Her pleasure turned him on. He had seemed to crave it, as if it was the ultimate in sensual gratification. He moved the way he had before, sitting up, holding her astride him on his lap. Face to face. Breath to breath.

'Then you came again.' He held her tight, one arm coiled around her waist, one hand on the back of her head. This was the ultimate in fantasy. She felt his body harden as she clung on to him.

'That one was softer. Longer. All over my body…' She couldn't describe it. A single tear rolled from her eye. She thought that had happened then, and that he'd kissed it away, just as he was doing now.

'I was trying to wait. I wanted to know if you were going for the hat-trick…' He chuckled quietly. 'But I couldn't.'

She'd felt him lose control, his strong body shaking, holding onto her as if she was the only thing in the world.

'How did it feel?' She wanted to share it with him again.

He shuddered, nuzzling at her neck. 'It felt like…being free.'

For a moment they were silent, just letting their hearts beat. Slowly, his hand moved for her breast, cupping it comfortably.

'You up to speed now?' His thumb grazed her nipple and her breath caught, tangled in pleasure. When he ran his tongue across her lips then kissed her again, sweet memories dissolved into anticipation.

'Hold me… Please, Drew.'

'I will.' The promise tore from his lips, and he twisted around, laying her down on the bed. She reached for the condoms on the nightstand, and he caught her hand. 'Not yet. Later.'

'Later?'

'Remember our agreement.'

She ran her finger over the magic marker on his arm. 'I don't need to remember it, I have it in writing.'

He grinned at her. 'Then you'll know we have a whole night. We can take our time.'

When the alarm went at five the following morning Sophie slept right through it, and Drew kissed her awake. There was no time for anything other than a quick dash to the shower and a grabbed cup of coffee, but that was okay. She'd be coming back home with him tonight, and there was no reason for them not to renew the contract that they'd washed off their arms in the shower this morning.

'I was thinking.' Sophie had decided to put the idea to him in the car so that they could talk about it. 'Why don't you take your bike off the lorry and ride it home while we're filming? Then you could get a taxi back to the hospital.' That would keep him out of the way for a while.

'Or I could do it while you're in Make-up. I'd be back mid-morning.'

'There's no rush. Why don't you have breakfast while I'm in Make-up and then—'

'You can kiss Todd while I'm out of the way?'

Sophie swallowed hard. 'There's that to it as well.'

'You'd feel better if I wasn't there?'

'How do you feel about it?'

There was silence for a couple of miles. It seemed they'd reached an impasse.

'Okay.' He spoke suddenly. 'Let's do this. I'll do what you said, stay until lunchtime and then take the bike home. When I get back, I'll be wanting a little reassurance, though.'

She grinned at him. 'You don't need any reassurance.' Last night had been all the reassurance that either of them could handle.

'I said *wanting*. Not *needing*.'

'Okay. Wanting's fine. In which case I might want a little reassurance back. Just because you do it so well.'

He laughed so hard that he nearly missed their turning. 'Yeah, okay. Flattery will get you everywhere.'

It had been a good day. She hadn't forgotten any of her lines, and the dozens of different disciplines that went into making a filmed sequence work had all fallen into place. She and Todd had clicked together and the gradually building tension, throughout the scene, had been almost palpable. Drew had good-naturedly disappeared after lunch, and she'd heard the roar of the engine as he'd revved the bike past the main entrance of the house.

It had been tiring, and it was almost good to feel this wrung out. She'd given it everything, and everyone had been pleased with the scene. Sophie walked back to her trailer and lay down on the couch, one arm slung over her eyes. She'd get changed out of her dress and take her make-up off in a moment.

Someone tapped on the door, and she answered automatically. Probably one of the wardrobe girls, or Jennie. If it was Jennie, she'd ask whether she'd seen Drew. It was getting late and she could do with going home soon.

'Hey.' His voice, the sound of the door closing, and a sharp click as the lock snapped fast. Sophie sat up.

'You're back.'

'I've been back a while. I took a walk around the grounds. I reckoned you were right in wanting me out of the way.'

'It's the best thing.'

He nodded. Approached her slowly. Suddenly she wasn't tired any more. Suddenly, every nerve was screaming for him. Particularly since she had a pretty good idea of what he was about to do.

Drew told himself that it was the damn costume. That the green and white print dress, ruched at the top to follow her curves, falling gently over her hips, was turning him into someone else. Someone who couldn't care less that they'd both had a long day. Someone who had conveniently forgotten that last night's promise must have expired by now.

He gathered her in his arms. When he kissed her he knew that the bright smear of lipstick, which made her mouth seem as luscious as ripened fruit, would be on his face too. The thought made him unexpectedly hard for her.

'Careful…' she murmured into his ear.

'Yeah.' He wondered whether she was in costume under that dress as well. He hoped so. He pushed her curled hair back from her neck and found a pin, holding it securely in place. A sudden whiff of Todd's aftershave.

'You smell of another man…' He kissed her neck, tenderly.

'You don't mind?' A little tremor of uncertainty racked her body, and then she relaxed into his arms. She seemed to understand that he couldn't have cared less.

'That wasn't real.' This was all-encompassingly real. It seemed the most genuine thing that had ever happened to him.

His hand skimmed the soft material of her dress and he gathered the fabric carefully in his hand, finding the edge of her stocking tops. Ran his finger around the place where flesh met nylon, feeling the depressions in her skin from the metal clips of her suspenders.

'You do this always? Wear the appropriate underwear?'

'It helps. You move differently…'

'Uh-huh.' He wondered how long it would take to get her out of the dress, undo the row of tiny buttons that ran down the side of it. Then there was the challenge of her underwear, unfamiliar hooks and fastenings and sheer stockings that mustn't be laddered by the clumsiness of his hands. The whole thing seemed impossibly impractical, and headily exciting.

His hands explored a little further, and found silky fabric, clinging to the rounded curve of her hips. He looked for buttons, elastic, something to give some clue about how to get her camiknickers off, and found nothing.

She was having more success. Her fingers loosened the belt of his jeans, and she slid her hand inside. When he felt her touch on his skin he groaned.

'I need some help with this, Sophie.' If he couldn't get inside her clothes soon, he was going to rip them off her.

'Where's the fun in that? Work it out for yourself.' She kissed him on the cheek, and he pulled her in for a proper kiss, his searching fingers dislodging a couple of bobby pins from her hair.

He was going to have to improvise. If his grandparents had managed this complex obstacle course, and his mere presence on this earth told Drew that they must have done at some point, then he ought to have a fighting chance. But he was going to need some help.

He backed her against the cupboard door, kissing her deep and hard, one hand over her breast. Gently, through the layers of fabric, he teased until her breathing started to quicken. He let the tension build, and when she moaned he left her with it, turning his attention to the buttons on her dress.

'Take it off…'

She responded to the low command, pulling the dress carefully over her head. Underneath, a lace-edged slip, the silken sheen of the material following her curves. He fell to one knee, sliding the fabric up her leg, kissing the inside of her thigh.

'Drew…' She whispered his name and the urgency in her voice almost destroyed him. He tried the camiknickers again, tugging gently downwards but there was still no give.

'How do I…?'

'Hooks and eyes.' Her hands went to her waist, and she unhooked the fastenings. Drew slid her silky knickers down, so she could step out of them.

That was enough. It was all his raging need would allow him to do. Reaching into his pocket, he found the condom he'd picked up earlier, thanking his lucky stars that he hadn't put it back into the box on his nightstand.

'Now… Please.' She pulled him to his feet, tugging at his jeans and dragging them far enough down to free him. He rolled the condom down in one swift movement, and then lifted her body, supporting her weight against the cupboard door. She wrapped her legs around his waist, moving against him.

Slow down. Show her some respect. His heart pounded as he nuzzled against her, opening her first with his fingers and then slipping inside. She cried out in frustration, moving against him, and he lost control.

'Yes…' She arched her back, not seeming to notice when she bumped her head on the cupboard door, and he curled one hand around the back of her skull to protect it. 'Again…'

He pulled out, then pushed inside her again. One hand flew to her mouth, smothering the cry that escaped her lips. He pulled back, knowing this time that this was what she wanted, making her wait as long as he could. At the next thrust, her body jerked in his arms and he was completely lost. Stripped of everything but the intense need that flashed between them.

'Not yet. Hold onto it, sweetheart.' He whispered the words into her ear. His body was doing everything to hers, driving her to completion, and yet still he wanted her to fight back against him.

'I can't…'

'Yes, you can. Make it last.' He knew that neither of them could hold out for long. But these moments of raw feeling were too good not to try.

In the few minutes before she came, she made him entirely hers. No thought left, hardly anything of him, apart from the need. When he felt her muscles tighten around him, all he could think of was that her pleasure seemed to be washing over him, possessing him. He had no chance to let go, she annihilated him, pulling the orgasm from him in waves of all-encompassing feeling.

For a couple of minutes they didn't move. Letting the shivered aftershocks rack their bodies, hearts beating fast against each other. She let out a little sigh and he kissed her.

'You okay, sweetheart?' He rested his forehead lightly against hers and she smiled.

'Much better than okay. Only I'll have to give you some lessons in vintage underwear. You're not quite as good with it as the modern stuff.'

'I'll practise.'

She laughed, kissing him lightly on the lips. 'Yeah. Practice makes perfect.'

CHAPTER FIFTEEN

IT WAS ALMOST as if he'd been gifted with another sense. One that knew whatever Sophie was feeling and whenever she needed him. On set, the smallest movement of her head made it obvious that she was about to ask for a break, and come to sit with him for a few minutes. In the evenings, the touch of her fingers on the back of his hand was enough to set his body on fire.

Possibly his favourite time of the day was when she got into the car with him at the end of the day. Smelling of soap, the lacquer brushed from her hair, and all his for the night.

'They've missed a bit.' Her hair was still slightly damp, and scraped back from her face, from where the make-up girls had cleaned off the fake blood that had spattered her in this afternoon's scene. A tiny red mark showed at her hairline and Drew leaned over to wipe it away.

She did what he'd been trying to avoid and reached forward, turning the rear-view mirror down to inspect the damage. 'No, that's a scar. From when I hit my head in the accident.'

Drew resigned himself to adjusting the mirror back again, and resolved for the hundredth time to leave a mirror in the glove compartment for her. Only she'd probably forget and still use his rear-view mirror whenever she wanted to check her appearance. The little routine, before he started the car, was more endearing and less annoying than he would have ever credited.

Something nagged at the back of his head as he drove. Something that formed itself into a concrete idea, which suddenly seemed so obvious that he could have kicked himself for not noticing before. He swung the car into a lay-by, and switched off the engine.

'That was where you banged your head?' He was thinking hard, trying not to jump to conclusions too fast.

'Yes, right here. I had bruises down the side of my face.' She reached for the rear-view mirror again, as if to check, and Drew caught her hand before she could get to it.

'And you had bruises on your shoulder?' He remembered that she had a thin red mark on one of her shoulders, the fading remains of a deep bruise, but his mind had been on other things when he'd last seen it.

She undid the top buttons of her shirt, pulling at the collar and squinting down at her shoulder. 'Right here. They were the two worst injuries.' She shivered, watching the traffic move past them on the road.

'Let me see…' He leaned over, running his finger along the tell-tale line, and she giggled.

'Not here…'

'Soph, that looks like a seat-belt injury.' He'd seen hundreds of such marks on crash victims, from where the seat belt had bitten into a shoulder. Right now he was kicking himself that this had never registered before.

'Yeah? I suppose so.' She still didn't see. 'It ran right across my shoulder.' She traced her finger in the exact line that Drew would have expected.

'And your car was a right-hand drive? Not a foreign import?'

'No, it was…' Suddenly light dawned in her eyes, and her hand flew to her mouth in shock. 'What are you saying?'

'That the location of your injuries suggests you were sitting on the opposite side of the car than you are now. Which is the driver's seat in the UK, but over in America…'

She caught her breath. 'It's the passenger seat. I must have banged my head on the inside of the car door.'

'Unless the impact crushed the cabin…' Drew was trying to ignore the excitement growing in his chest, take in all the possibilities. Right now there was nothing on her right side that she could have bumped her head on, but a crash could do anything to a car's frame.

'No… No, it didn't. I saw the pictures on the police report, I've got them somewhere. The front of the car had been staved in, but I remember thinking how lucky we were that the inside of the car was practically untouched… Drew…' She turned towards him, tears melting her eyes into soft focus.

He dared say the unthinkable. The impossible, and yet yearned-for truth. 'It looks as if you weren't driving…' If Josh had lied about that, then what else had he lied about?

She looked around, as if his own car could provide her with some answers. 'Can we prove it?'

'I don't know. Maybe. If I could get the report from the doctor who saw you at the hospital right after the crash, there might be some notes. He might even have mentioned a seat-belt injury, they're very common.' Drew bit back his own enthusiasm. 'It may be nothing, Soph. We might never be able to say for sure.'

'But there's a doubt. A possibility.' She snapped open her seat belt and flung her arms around his shoulders. She buried her head in his shoulder. 'Why does this mean so much to me?'

'If Josh lied about this, maybe he lied about other things. You don't have to just believe his version of events, you can make your own decision.'

'Yes… That's it. He…' She seemed to pull herself together a little, relaxing in his arms. 'He had points on his licence. He would have been banned from driving if he was in another accident. Maybe I agreed to switch places with him.'

'Maybe you did. Or maybe he saw that you were disorientated after the accident and took a chance, reckoning you wouldn't disagree with him. That's not what really matters, though, is it?'

'No, it's not. He painted me as a monster, and now one part of his story doesn't hold up. Maybe I'm not so bad…' She started to tremble, as if on the verge of an explosion of tears.

'You're not so bad. Trust me. I don't need to know whether you were driving or not to believe that.'

'Thank you.' She stretched up to kiss him, her lips like the whisper of a summer breeze on his. 'I think I'll have to think about this all over again.'

'You do that.' Drew waited for her to sit back into her seat and buckle her seat belt. 'Is it your turn to cook tonight?'

'Probably.' She reached for her notebook and consulted the pages. 'Yep. I'm doing fajitas.'

'Great.' He reached for the ignition. 'You can think while you're cooking.'

She knew what she needed to do. When they arrived home Sophie spied her laptop on the coffee table in the sitting-room, and made for it. The pictures still felt like unfinished business. She needed to show them to Drew, before either of them could move on.

'It's time we looked, Drew.' She plumped herself down on the sofa, blinking as the screen in front of her lit up, and wishing that the gazillion-colour picture quality wasn't quite so well engineered.

He seemed to know what she had on her mind. 'Soph, you don't have to…'

'I want to.' This was the test. Whether he had enough confidence in her to look at the pictures, or whether he would just bury his head in the sand, hoping they'd go away.

'Okay.' He sat down next to her, stretching his arm across the cushions behind her. Sophie opened the folder, hidden deep in the warren of files, and typed the password. Five tiny icons appeared in the corner of the screen, which gave no good idea of the photographs they represented.

'Ready?'

'I'm ready. If you are.'

She ignored the implicit question. She was never going to be ready for this, not if she lived to be a hundred. She doubted if Drew really knew what he was saying either, but this was the only way forward.

The first photo wasn't too bad. It would actually have been quite a good one, if taken on its own, Sophie curled up on a bed in a plush hotel room, the sheet that covered her following the contours of her body.

'Okay. That's not so bad…' His fingers found her shoulder, giving it a reassuring squeeze.

'They get worse.'

'Yeah. I'd figured that out.'

In the next, the sheet had been drawn back. She was lying on her right side, but the bruise on her shoulder was just visible, half-obscured by pillows. She felt his body stiffen against hers.

'I…' When she looked round at him, his face had gone suddenly pale. Sophie wondered if he had the same punched-in-the-gut feeling that she'd had when she'd first seen the photos. 'Zoom in a bit…on the bruise…'

If that was the way he wanted to play it. Just look at her shoulder, nothing else. Step back from the rest of it. She magnified the photo, thinking grimly that it must be high resolution, because the quality hardly deteriorated.

'That's… It looks like a seat-belt injury to me. From… what I can see.'

She took a deep breath. 'Next one?'

He didn't reply. Just nodded. In the next photo, she was lying on her back, her hair obscuring the right side of her face, her shoulder out of the view of the camera. Sophie wondered whether he would notice that her nipples were hardened into tight points, as if someone had just been touching them.

A soft curse, under his breath. Yeah. He'd noticed.

'I'm sorry, Drew.'

'Don't… It's not your fault.' His arm finally wound around her shoulder, and she felt herself shudder in response to that small comfort. 'Soph, I'm so sorry this happened to you.'

He was drawing back. Protecting himself from it all. She'd known he must, and all she could do was hope that when he'd thought about it, he'd still be able to touch her. Her fingers were trembling, and she completely missed the next icon and clicked by mistake on the last, and worst, of them.

She heard him catch his breath. She was still lying on her back, her hair still flopped over her right eye, but her face betrayed a languid smile. It was the kind of pose that a model might strike to suggest sex.

But this was obviously not posed. Drew had been humiliated once by photographs, and these *had* to be worse than the ones of his ex-girlfriend.

She turned to look at him. His eyes were dead, staring at the screen, a look of sheer rage on his face.

'I'm sorry. I'm so sorry, Drew.' She slammed the lid of her laptop shut, trying to break the noxious spell, but still it seemed to linger.

'It's…okay, Soph.' She felt his hand, cold on hers.

He pulled her to her feet and her laptop slipped from her lap, sliding onto the carpet. Hugged her tightly. Sophie waited for the warmth, the enveloping feeling that everything was all right, and it didn't come. His hands were planted on her back, still and lifeless. It was as if she were being embraced by a tailor's dummy.

'Drew… Please…' She just wanted to sink into his arms, feel the forgiveness that his words had volunteered. But she couldn't. She'd pushed him too far, and Drew was a man, and a human being. This was too much for him.

'It's okay, Soph. Really. They're a shock, but...'

I still love you. Say it. Say it.

'We'll get over this.'

'Yeah. We will.' Or maybe not. Drew was steeped in his work and his good reputation. This must be sheer torture for him.

'Why don't I go and make dinner?' It was all she could think of, to bring them both back to normality a little.

'Yeah. Okay.' He agreed a bit too fast. 'I might go for a run, if that's okay with you...?'

He'd never asked before. Just changed into his sweats, bade her a cheery goodbye, and left her to get on with whatever she was doing. Things were different now.

'Be back for dinner. In an hour.'

'Of course.' Finally he smiled. Somehow it was the worst of it all. He was making an effort to be nice, but Sophie knew that he was angry with her. She was never going to be rid of those damn photographs. And now they'd driven Drew away.

Even running, as hard and fast as he could, couldn't get rid of it. The anger that someone could do this to Sophie. When he got to the park, Drew dropped for a punishing round of push-ups, which only served to make his shoulders ache and didn't dispel the rage.

They ate together, talking and laughing. Sophie's laugh seemed somehow brittle tonight, as if she was having to put on an act. Still the anger burned.

When he'd finished stacking the dishwasher, he made coffee for himself and herbal tea for her. She sipped it in silence and then went to bed early, leaving Drew to plot the most horrible revenge he could think of against the man who'd done this to her.

That didn't work either, and when he slid between the

sheets she was curled up, fast asleep. He kissed her brow and rolled onto his back, to stare impotently up at the darkness.

They were both groggy and tired the next morning. Drew hadn't slept much, and he wondered whether Sophie's regular breathing in the bed beside him had been just a pretence of sleep. Perhaps he should have made the effort to rouse her, and to talk to her, but he wasn't sure what he could possibly have said. Just that this hurt, but she knew that already, better than he did.

The weather was forecast as fine for the next week, and Joel had decided to shoot the scenes at the lake that lay in the grounds of Hazlemere House. Drew followed a makeshift sign along a gravelled road and parked next to Sophie's trailer, where Jennie was waiting for them.

In the last month, Jennie's job had suddenly become less fraught. Drew knew that Sophie had apologised to her for her behaviour, without going into any details, and the easier relationship showed in Jennie's smile.

'We're not late, are we?' Sophie seemed on edge this morning.

'No, there's plenty of time. But whenever you're ready for Wardrobe and Make-up…'

'I'm ready now. Thanks, Jennie.'

'I'll catch you later, down by the lake. I'm going to look at this submersible…' He was aware that the smile he gave her felt awkward on his lips.

'Yes. Later.'

Everyone knew him by now, either as a set advisor, the doctor who was useful to have around for minor bumps and sprains, or the guy who always seemed to be somewhere near Sophie. No one seemed to care much which of those hats he was wearing at any given time, and Drew received waves and nods of acknowledgement as he walked down to the lake.

A small jetty reached out into the expanse of shimmering

water, a square platform at the end. The timbers looked old, but when he craned to see underneath, he could see fresh wood. The whole thing had been built especially and aged to look as if it had been there for a while.

Next to the jetty a small metal craft bobbed in the water. The submersible. Drew had seen the cramped inside of it built in a warehouse in Devon, and had marvelled at the bravery of going underwater in such a thing. Now the craft looked even tinier and more precariously dangerous.

The early morning chill still hung in the air, and he pulled his jacket around him, settling himself in a seat. Sophie was called straight from Make-up down onto the jetty to go through her scene with Todd. Today she was wearing a red dress with a grey knitted cardigan, her legs bare.

Joel was placing all the actors, marking out their positions on the jetty, supervising the camera angles and checking the direction of the light. So many details that went into just a few minutes of filming. The actors ran through the scene one last time, and then came the moment that was beginning to excite Drew as much as it seemed to thrill everyone else on the set. In response to a call for silence, the bustle quietened and the cameras were ready to roll.

Cups of tea and the inevitable doughnuts. More debate over camera angles, and the sun climbing in the sky began to make Drew feel sleepy. A boom was rigged up on the jetty so that the cameraman could swing out over the water and film the conversation taking place in a small rowing boat, next to the submersible. Sophie joined him to watch for a few minutes and then was called back for one of her scenes.

A shout from the waterside made him jump, dropping his book. Then a scream, which drove him to his feet before he knew what was happening. The boom was sagging over the water, the three men who had been providing a counterbalance for the long arm grappling to control it. But all he could see was Sophie.

He ran. There was only one place that he belonged now,

and that was at the end of the jetty, where Sophie was calling to the cameraman, who was fighting to keep his balance on the other end of the swaying boom.

'Sophie, get out of the way...'

She either didn't hear him or she was ignoring him. Drew pushed through the crowd that was milling around at the waterside and made a spurt of speed along the jetty.

'Joe... Your safety harness...' Sophie was standing still, perilously close to the swinging arm of the boom.

If the boom collapsed into the water, taking Joe with it, he would be trapped. Drew saw Joe respond to Sophie's words, unclipping his harness from the frame.

'Get out of the way...' He grabbed her, pulling her clear of the boom, and when she struggled he picked her up bodily. Joe chose that moment to jump into the water, and now that it no longer supported his weight, the boom shot upwards, slewing violently.

'He's in the water...'

'I know. I'll get him. Stay there.' He dumped her back onto her feet, out of the reach of the boom, and Drew kicked off his shoes.

'Get everyone off the jetty...' Someone had called for a lifebuoy, but no one seemed to know where they were. A couple of men were wading into the water from the shore, but Drew was closer to Joe, who was struggling in the deep water, weighed down by the heavy safety harness.

'Go, Sophie.'

She hesitated, seemingly confused for a moment and about to panic. Then she turned, shouting to the people around them to get back, moving with them to safety, as Drew dived into the lake.

He reached Joe before any of the other men in the water, catching his flailing arm and supporting him while he punched the release for the harness and got him out of it. It was easier now to keep him afloat, and together the two men swam for the shore.

'Okay, mate?' Joe was breathing heavily, stumbling out of the water, but there was no blood and he seemed uninjured. Willing hands supported him onto the grass, to sit down and catch his breath.

'Yeah. Thanks…' Joe's head swivelled round in response to a shout, and Drew followed his gaze. Everyone was off the jetty now, apart from a young woman, one of the sound technicians, who was sprinting to the far end of it. And Sophie had left the safety of the water's edge and was running after her.

'Theresa… Leave it…' Sophie's voice floated across to him in the sudden hush.

Dammit! When he'd told Sophie to get everyone off the jetty, he'd taken it for granted that she'd include herself in that instruction. Theresa had reached the end now and was struggling to pull a heavy metal trunk, containing sound equipment, back to safety.

'Duck…' He shouted the word as a sudden gust of wind blew the boom around almost full circle. Sophie hit the deck, but Theresa ignored him, and the boom caught her, propelling both her and the equipment she'd tried to save into the water.

'Soph…' He was running now, as if his own life depended on it. Sophie had got to her hands and knees and was crawling towards the edge of the jetty to see what had become of Theresa. Then she seemed to tip over, letting herself down into the lake.

Sophie. Sophie. Drew saw the bright flash of her hair in the water, and then she bobbed beneath the surface. He dived in after her.

At first he couldn't see them. Then a shadow, moving under the water. Her blonde hair had broken free of the pins that had held it and was streaming behind her. Taking a deep breath, he dived, feeling the water sting his eyes. It was hard to see, but then he found what he was looking for. Sophie's frightened face, streams of bubbles rising from her mouth from the effort of trying to pull Theresa's limp body to the surface.

He grabbed her arm, motioning her out of the way, and she shot upwards, towards the glow of the sunshine above their heads. No longer trapped in the all-encompassing noise of instinctive fear for Sophie, he reached for Theresa.

She seemed to be trapped somehow, and he worked his way down to her legs. One was pinned between the underwater timbers of the jetty and the metal trunk that had fallen into the lake. He tugged at the trunk, the handles tearing into his fingers.

It didn't budge. He braced his legs against the trunk and his shoulder against the jetty and pushed as hard as he could, feeling a sudden sharp pain in his shoulder as his foot slipped and he crashed against the timbers. It was enough, though. Theresa's leg shifted and he saw her body moving upwards in a motion that was almost purposeful. When he looked, he saw that Sophie was there again, her arms around Theresa's shoulders, lifting her up towards the light.

Three heads broke the surface almost at the same time. Two sets of aching lungs gasped for air and the third, Theresa's, couldn't respond. Sophie was struggling to keep her afloat, a dead weight in the water, and Drew took over. Pain shot through his left shoulder and along his arm as he tried to swim and he heard a sickening crunch as the bones relocated into their proper alignment.

Somehow, he and Sophie managed to get Theresa back to the men who were waiting for them, waist deep in the water. Strong arms hoisted her clear, and carried her back to the shore.

'She's dead… She's dead…' he heard a woman sob as he stumbled out of the water, Sophie by his side. Not yet. Not if he had anything to do with it.

'Out of the way.' He heard Sophie's voice, calm and assertive, cutting through the pain.

'Call an ambulance.' Jennie was on hand, as always, and

she pulled her phone from her pocket in response to his words. 'Give me some space...'

A small circle formed around Theresa's lifeless body. 'Ian, we need the first-aid kit. Andrew, get a blanket to keep her warm.' Sophie took the words from his mouth, assigning tasks to the people she knew would complete them with the minimum of fuss.

He knelt down next to Theresa, clearing her mouth and tipping her head to one side and then back ready for CPR, using his uninjured left arm as much as possible. Pinching her nose, he delivered two rescue breaths and then cried out in agony as he tried to move on to the compressions.

'I'll do it.' Sophie was kneeling on the other side of Theresa's motionless body, her wet hair pushed back from her face.

'Can you...?' There was no point in asking, really. Drew didn't have the strength in his arm and couldn't keep up the rhythmic, lifesaving effort that was needed.

'Count for me.' She positioned her body over Theresa's the way he'd seen her do with the dummy, and Drew wrenched his consciousness away from the screaming pain in his shoulder and concentrated on counting, keeping the beat of the compressions for her.

He could use his left hand, as long as he didn't try to raise his arm. After thirty compressions, he delivered two rescue breaths. Repeat. Repeat.

'It's not working...' Sophie ignored the words behind her, and so did Drew. Another repeat. Then Theresa choked, water and vomit bubbling from her mouth.

Sophie wasn't prepared for this. She'd listened well when her father had taught her the basics of first aid, resuscitation, how to stop bleeding. It had all been precious time with him, and she'd practised on her own afterwards, wanting to gain his approval with her willingness to learn.

She knew exactly how to deliver the compressions and rescue breaths. But dummies didn't vomit all over you.

She helped Drew roll Theresa onto her side, and he bent over, clearing her mouth with his finger. Then a tight smile twitched at his lips.

'Theresa. Theresa… It's all right, sweetheart. Just breathe. You're all right.'

She saw Theresa's arms twitch in an involuntary movement. Then a choking sound and another wheezing breath. And another. She heard the sound of someone crying behind her, and realised that her own face was wet with tears.

Drew was talking to Theresa, watching her reactions. Then his gaze flipped up to Sophie, and he nodded, a smile in his eyes.

'I need you to help me a bit more.' His voice had the same reassuring tone that he'd been using with Theresa.

'Okay, no problem.' She steeled herself, trying to stop shaking. 'What's wrong with your arm?' She couldn't see any blood on him.

'I think I knocked it out slightly. It's okay, I felt it snap back again.'

Sophie rolled her eyes but his gaze was already back on Theresa. As soon as she was safe and on her way to hospital Sophie was going to make him sit down and take notice of her. In the meantime, all she could do was to follow his instructions to the letter.

'Wash your hands.' She looked down at her own hands, realised they were covered with vomit and grabbed at the water bottle lying on the grass nearby. 'Look in the first-aid kit. Get a pair of gloves for yourself, and a pair for me. Find something to wipe Theresa's face with.'

He gave the instructions quietly, one at a time, waiting for her to do each thing before he went on to the next. She could do this. He was there, he wouldn't let her forget anything, or do something wrong.

She rolled up a towel, slipping it under Theresa's head as he told her. Andrew was deputised to watch Theresa, hold her hand and call out immediately if she gave any signs of distress, and Sophie covered her with a blanket, tucking it carefully around her.

'Have we got an ambulance coming?' he called to the group behind them, and Jennie answered.

'Yes. It'll be twenty minutes before they get here, though, they're a way off.'

'All right. Keep me posted.' Drew turned his attention back to Theresa, who had begun to moan, her free hand seeming to reach downwards. 'Steady, sweetheart. Try to lie still.'

Theresa didn't respond, a keening cry escaping her lips. Drew's mouth tightened into a thin line. 'Andrew, keep her still if you can. Sophie, I need you to help me.'

Quietly, he talked her through it, helping with his one good hand wherever he could. Loosening Theresa's clothes to look at her chest and stomach, to check that there were no injuries there. Sophie could already see that Theresa's left leg was swelling under the thin material of her wide-legged trousers.

'You've seen her leg?'

He nodded. 'First things first.'

She remembered that. Breathing. Then bleeding. Stomach and chest injuries first. Sophie took a deep breath and went through the checks, one by one.

'Still with me?' His voice again. Not tender. Not even kind, but there was something else there that made her strong. When she looked up at his face she saw it. A confident half-smile that told her he was in no doubt about whether she could do this or not.

'Like your shadow.' She smiled back.

He reached for the first-aid box, pulling it towards him and taking a pair of scissors out. Carefully, he cut the wide leg of Theresa's trousers, and she helped him to lift it slightly to see underneath, where the centre of the swelling seemed to be.

'What is it?' She'd craned around in an attempt to see

what Drew saw, without getting in his way. The whole of Theresa's calf was swollen and a blotchy red colour, with what looked like small blisters forming on the surface of the skin. 'A jellyfish?'

He shook his head. 'Her leg's obviously taken a pretty hard blow at some point. Could be that there's a break in one of the blood vessels.'

'Internal bleeding.' Sophie whispered the words, almost to herself. They didn't sound good.

'I'll need to make sure there's nothing else.' His gaze flipped to Theresa's face as she moaned and tried to move and Andrew soothed her, stroking her hair. 'I want you to hold her leg still for me while I do it.'

'Okay. Show me where…'

His words guided her hands and she gently supported the leg, clear of the sand beneath it, concentrating on keeping it still. Drew craned round, looking at it carefully.

'The blisters, Drew…' A long blister seemed to have formed before her very eyes, running down the back of Theresa's leg.

'Yeah. I don't want to drain it here, that needs to be done in sterile conditions.' He looked up. 'Ambulance?'

'Ten minutes…' Jennie's voice again.

'Let's hope so.' His whispered words came through gritted teeth and a cold feeling of dread crawled across her skin. What if it was more? What if he was going to need her to cut the leg, to drain it?

If she had to do it, she would. Drew wouldn't let her fail. She moved automatically, responding to Drew's instructions, carefully cleaning the detritus of the lake away as best she could and wrapping a large dressing pad loosely around it. Drew folded a soft quilted jacket that someone had produced, sliding it underneath and covering it with a towel.

'Okay. That's enough. Just lay her leg down carefully.'

Theresa was shifting restlessly, trying to move, and Drew

inched sideways. 'Theresa… Listen, honey, I know your leg is hurting you.'

'Yeah.' Theresa was crying softly. 'Is it broken?'

'No, but you've taken a blow to the back of your leg and it's quite swollen. There's an ambulance on its way and you're going to be just fine.' He waited for Theresa's nod and gave her a melting smile. 'Hang on in there, okay?'

'Yeah. Okay.'

'Can we give her something for the pain? I've got some aspirins in my bag,' Sophie whispered to Drew when he turned his attention back to her. 'Wherever it is…' She didn't have the faintest idea, but she had a good enough excuse for losing it and expected that Jennie would be able to find it.

'No, giving her anything aspirin based is only going to make the bleeding worse. The ambulance paramedics will be far better equipped to deal with that when they get here.' His gaze found hers. Sure and steady, melting away at the edges of her fear. The sound of a distant siren floated in on the breeze.

'Here they are…'

He nodded. 'Yeah. It's time for you to step back now.' He turned, beckoning to Jennie. 'Go with Jennie and let her get you into some dry clothes.'

'But you—'

'I'll be with you as soon as I can. I need to talk to the paramedics when they arrive.'

'You're not going in the ambulance.'

He shook his head. 'I can't help them, and I'll just be in the way.'

She frowned at him. 'That's not what I meant. I meant you need a doctor to have a look at *you*.'

'It's okay. I dislocated my shoulder when I was a kid. I banged it underwater, and it slipped out very slightly and then back in again. I just need to rest up a bit.' He turned to Jennie. 'Will you get some warm clothes and a blanket for Sophie, please? Make sure she sits down and has a hot drink.'

'Gotcha.' Jennie held out her hand to help Sophie to her feet, and she ignored it.

She didn't want to leave him now. She didn't want to leave Theresa. She couldn't. She was sure that if she went along to the hospital there was something that she could do.

'Stepping back's the hardest thing, Soph. You have to do it now, because if you don't you'll be in the way.' His voice *was* tender now. Full of everything that she felt, and everything that he knew.

'Come on, Sophie.' Jennie bent down, taking her by the shoulders, trying to avoid the bits of her dress that were stained with vomit. Numbly she got to her feet.

'I'll see you soon?' She could see the ambulance crew now, walking towards them.

'I'll be right there.'

She allowed Jennie to lead her away, but suddenly clean clothes weren't uppermost in her mind. She broke away from her, gagging as she ran to the water's edge, and then retching violently into the water.

CHAPTER SIXTEEN

DREW HAD BROUGHT the ambulance paramedics up to date, and they'd carried Theresa to the ambulance, making her comfortable for the ride to the hospital. Andrew climbed in to go with her, and she managed a small smile and a wave in Drew's direction. Then he made himself do what he'd told Sophie to do, and turned away.

His shoulder throbbed mercilessly. He should find a sling, that would make it more comfortable while he rested it up for the next couple of days. Easy enough, this had happened before a couple of times, and he knew exactly what to do.

But first he had to find Sophie. He wanted to make sure that she was all right, and that she was out of her wet clothes. He walked quickly to her trailer, tapping on the door and grunting with pain as he automatically reached for the handle with his left hand.

Inside, Sophie was showered and dressed, sitting down and protesting as Jennie tried to wrap a blanket around her.

'He said blanket. Clean clothes, hot drink and a blanket…' Stress showed in Jennie's face as the conflict between following a star's every command and doing as the doctor said seemed to overwhelm her.

'Nice going, Jennie.' Drew grinned at her and Jennie relaxed a bit.

'Drew. Sit down.' Sophie lost interest in the blanket, and Jennie surreptitiously tucked it over her legs. When he didn't obey straight away her face took on a determined look. 'Sit, will you?'

'Feeling better?' Out of the corner of his eye he'd seen Sophie run to the water's edge and throw up, then allow Jennie to lead her away.

'Yes.' She dismissed his enquiry with an imperious wave of her hand. She obviously *was* feeling better. 'Jennie, can you get some dry clothes for Drew, please? And a triangular bandage from the first-aid kit.'

'Right.' Jennie brightened considerably at the prospect of a task that didn't involve blankets.

'And some paracetamol, if you can find any.' Drew lowered himself slowly into a seat.

'Sure thing. How many?'

'Bring me the packet.' He might well need some more for later. Jennie disappeared, and Sophie fixed him with a glare. 'Well?'

'Well, what?' He was beginning to shiver now, his wet clothes sticking to his skin.

'Are you going to do as *I* tell you now?'

He'd thought about getting her to lie down for a while and waiting until she had recovered enough for him to scold her for running back down that damn jetty and putting herself deliberately in danger. But right now his whole body ached, and the thing he most wanted was for Sophie to hold him.

'Yeah. Okay.'

She helped him out of his clothes, and shepherded him into the tiny shower cubicle at the other end of the trailer. Rolled her sleeves up and soaped him clean, then dried him and wrapped a large towel securely around his waist, leading him through to the seating area.

'Where's Jennie got to?' She peered through the window.

'Soph...'

'They must have something in your size. What's the point

of having a wardrobe department if they can't rustle up some dry clothes?'

'Soph…' He reached for her and she turned, her vexed expression softening suddenly. 'Sophie, come here.'

She walked towards him, and he wound his good arm around her waist, pulling her close. She hugged him awkwardly, trying not to touch his injured shoulder, ending up holding his head to her chest. That was okay. That was right where he wanted to be. He could hear her heart beating, smell the delicate perfume of her body.

'I'm so cross with you…'

'I know. I know, the photographs.'

'What? No!' Was that really what she'd thought? 'Sophie I was angry *for* you. Not *with* you. How could you have thought…?'

She shrugged wordlessly. Of course she'd thought that his anger had been directed at her. Everyone else seemed to blame her for the images.

'Soph. I'm sorry. Why on earth didn't you say something?'

'I was hoping you'd come around. That you might think they weren't so bad after all.'

'They're horrible. I hate them, because they hurt you, and because people think that they're your fault in some way. That's all. You have nothing to apologise for.'

She seemed almost breathless with relief. 'So why are you cross with me, then?'

For a moment Drew couldn't think. 'Oh. Yes, I'm cross with you for running down that jetty. Putting yourself in danger.' He tugged her closer, wincing as pain shot through his shoulder. He didn't care. Only Sophie mattered.

'Oh. Well, I'm not sorry for that.'

'No, I didn't think you would be.' This was *his* Sophie. Spirited and brave, a woman with her own opinions. Not the bullied, frightened person who either lashed out or apologised for everything.

'We did okay, didn't we?'

'A lot better than okay. You helped save a life.'

She nodded. 'That feels good. I'm so proud of you, Drew.'

His heart warmed and he held her close, catching his breath as he pulled her against his injured arm. 'I'm always proud of you. Most especially today.'

She bent, kissing his forehead, a tear rolling down her cheek and splashing onto his. 'Thank you. That means a great deal.'

A tap sounded on the door of the trailer and Sophie backed away from him quickly, rubbing her face with her sleeve. 'Come in…'

Jennie appeared, a bundle of things in her arms. 'Clothes.' She draped a pair of combat trousers and a T-shirt over the back of a chair. 'I found your shoes on the end of the jetty. Triangular bandage.' She fished in her pocket for something. 'And some safety pins.'

'Thanks, Jennie.' When Drew reached for the bandage, Sophie picked it up. 'Did you find any paracetamol?'

'Yeah.' Jennie gave the packet to Sophie, and Drew realised that there wasn't much point in trying to take control here. She squinted at the instructions.

'A thousand milligrams.' He prompted her with the dose.

She broke two tablets out of the foil, letting him see the label on the packet. Sixteen five-hundred-milligram tablets. Put the tablets into his hand and the packet into her handbag. Drew grinned. No one, *no one* else would have got to do that with him. Except Sophie.

He downed the tablets and she handed him a glass of water. Drew took a couple of gulps and handed it back to her. If she wanted to play nurse then she could put the glass back on the table. He wondered vaguely whether she'd consider giving him a massage later.

'We're going to be breaking for the day now?' Sophie turned to Jennie.

'Yes. They'll have the set builders in tonight, repairing

the damage, and Joel's sending in the second crew to film the shots of the submersible going up and down tomorrow. There are a couple more things he needs you and Todd for, and he'll do those tomorrow afternoon.'

'So we get a lie-in?' Sophie grinned.

'Yep. Would you like me to get one of the drivers to take you home?'

'Thanks. I think it would be better if Drew didn't drive tonight, at least.'

'I'll find someone.' Jennie disappeared, and as soon as the door of the trailer slammed behind her Drew had Sophie back in his arms again.

'Are you going to help me on with my clothes now?'

She giggled. 'That'll be a first. I suppose it's just the same as helping you off with them, only in reverse.'

'I expect so. And then home.'

She nodded. 'Yeah. Home. That would be just wonderful.'

CHAPTER SEVENTEEN

THE WEEKS THAT had stretched out ahead of them began to trickle away and became days. Ten days before they were due to wrap the film it was announced that they'd made good progress and should be finished in seven. Sophie wanted to personally shake everyone on set who'd worked so hard to deprive her of three precious days.

That evening she told Drew that she was tired and went to bed early. When he padded quietly into the room and slipped under the duvet next to her, she pretended to be asleep. It was another night wasted from their precious, ever-dwindling supply, but she couldn't fake it. If she let him hold her, let him make love to her, she wouldn't be able to stop herself from crying.

When the alarm went the following morning she got out of bed and locked herself in the bathroom, staring into the mirror. Today was their last day in London, and tomorrow they'd travel up to Bath to shoot the final scenes. Then the end-of-shoot party. They still had six days, and she should make the most of them.

When she went downstairs Drew kissed her as if nothing was wrong, and she kissed him back. They talked in the car on the way to the set, and she tried to laugh, even managing it a few times. Today was going to be a good day. She'd make it so.

It was a long day, Joel making sure that they had everything they needed before they had to leave the Hertfordshire set. Drew sat in on the shooting as usual, there to help her through if she needed it. Sophie almost wished that she did need him, but somehow even her unpredictable memory chose today to retain every single word of the script.

They got back to his house at ten in the evening. 'I can't wait to just soak in a hot bath…' Sophie made for the stairs.

'Can we stay here a moment?' He opened the door to the sitting-room. 'There's something I want to talk about.'

The arrangements for travelling to Bath tomorrow maybe. Whatever it was, he didn't look particularly happy about it.

'What is it?' Sophie followed him into the sitting-room and perched on the edge of the sofa. Something was wrong, she could feel it, buzzing in the air between them.

'Carly's going to be coming by in the morning.'

'Yes, I know.' Carly had decided to fly back for the last week of shooting and the end-of-shoot party. In reality, Sophie suspected that decision had been made with Drew, and that it had something to do with making sure that she got back to America in one piece. Right now, she was tempted to tell him that he didn't need to have bothered about that. She wasn't going.

A thought suddenly hit Sophie. 'She's all right isn't she?'

'Carly's fine. She got an earlier plane and landed this morning. I spoke to her today.'

'Why didn't she call me?' Something was going on. Both Carly and Drew were in on it, and it wasn't good. 'Stop beating around the bush, Drew, and tell me.'

'I'm not coming with you to Bath.'

'What?' She felt sick. She knew the answer to the next question, but there was no way she could prevent herself from asking it. No way that she could roll time back and not have this conversation. 'Why?'

'Because we've come to the end of things. We've already

taken as much as we can from this relationship, and there just isn't anything more.'

He might have come to the end of it, but she hadn't. There was still so much more she wanted to do with him.

'You're wrong.'

'Maybe. But I've made my decision. I'm not coming with you to Bath.'

'Then I'll come back here in a week's time. We can decide what to do then.' All Sophie's thoughts were beginning to splinter in her head. Everything was shattering around her. She willed herself to breath, to hold on. She couldn't lose it now.

'It's not just a matter of geography, Sophie. I'm ending this now.'

'Well, you can't. What about me? Don't I have a say in it?'

He shook his head slowly. Of course she didn't. If one partner wanted to end things then the other one just had to put up with it.

'At least tell me why. I deserve that, don't I?'

Something softened in his eyes. For a moment she thought that he was going to relent. He'd examined the reason and found it wanting.

'I'm a doctor, Sophie. I give a lot of time to my work, it's what I am. Who I am.'

'And you can't be seen with me, is that it?' Cold dread crept over her. This was the one thing that she could never change about herself. Her past. Everything she touched would be tainted by it.

'Your life and mine…they're different. I can't give up my career and follow you, Sophie. I thought that none of it was worth anything any more, and then I met you and you taught me different.'

'Who said you had to give it up?' It was make or break now. Dammit, it wasn't going to be break. 'I'll retire.'

'Don't be ridiculous. You're twenty-eight years old.'

'Yeah, well, they say that you don't get the parts when you get past forty.' She shrugged. Was it really that easy? Allow her whole career to dissolve with a shrug of her shoulders?

'No. I won't let you.'

'You don't have any choice in the matter. You don't get to say what I do with *my* career.'

'Exactly. And you don't get to say what I do with mine either. We can't be together because we have different lives. We're different people.'

'You want me to beg? Is that it?' She would. Five minutes of his time every day, that was all she wanted. Five minutes and the chance to sleep beside him.

'No!' He turned on her, rage showing in his face. 'You should never beg, Sophie. Never.'

Something cold settled around her heart, like frost in July. 'Fine. Then I won't.'

She turned and marched out of the room. Drew didn't think that she was good enough for him. He hadn't said it, but he hadn't denied it either. He got to have his photo in respectable magazines, and hers was plastered up on the internet and in scandal sheets. *That* was what he meant by *different people*.

He didn't even try to stop her. In that moment she knew that he wouldn't stop her from leaving tomorrow either.

He wasn't there the following morning. Or in the other bedroom. When Sophie crept downstairs she saw cushions and a blanket scattered on the sofa, and heard the noise of the shower downstairs in the utility room next to the garage.

She showered and got dressed, applying her make-up carefully. She knew Drew well enough to know that he wouldn't have changed his mind. That he thought this was the right thing to do and would remain steadfast. Maybe he was right. She'd made the decision years ago that she didn't want to live the way her mother did, never knowing when her father was going to come home.

Even so, walking out of here with Carly, leaving him behind, was going to have to be the best performance of her life. She applied a little more blusher and then wiped it off. Against the paleness of her face, and her hollow eyes, it looked like red cheeks painted on a doll.

She heard the doorbell, and Drew answered it. Carly's voice and then footsteps on the stairs. The bedroom door opened.

'You okay?' Carly walked into the room. Tanned and frowning.

'Yes. You?'

'Me? I'm fine. Tired of sitting around doing nothing.' Carly came forward for a hug, and Sophie clung to her.

'So, we're off, then?' Sophie tried to smile and wondered if it was as brittle as her voice sounded.

'Don't you want to say goodbye to him?' Carly's face was suddenly tender.

'I… No. I don't think I can say goodbye to him.' That would break her. Maybe if there were no goodbyes, she could pretend that she might see him again.

'Okay. Finish getting ready, and I'll throw the rest of your stuff into a case. We can sort it all out when we get to Bath.'

When Sophie took a deep breath and went downstairs, Drew wasn't there. She could see him sitting in the kitchen, the door open, watching for her, but she turned away and he didn't move. She carried her case out to the car and put it into the boot.

Carly had stopped in the doorway with the smaller case, and was looking back into the house. Drew appeared next to her, and they exchanged a couple of words. Then he bent, kissing her on the cheek, and Carly hugged him.

Sophie knew that he was watching as they lifted the second case into the boot and got into the car. When she finally looked behind her, she could see him at the end of the path, hands in his pockets, watching the car disappear along the road.

'I'm not heartless.' Carly must think she was a monster for not even saying goodbye. 'He ended it.'

'I know. He told me that.'

'He did?'

'Yep. He said that you weren't to blame for anything.'

An agonised wail, which didn't seem to belong to her, rose from her throat. Carly stopped the car and hugged her, while Sophie cried on her shoulder.

CHAPTER EIGHTEEN

THE LAST MONTH had been a whirl of activity. Almost since her plane had touched down Sophie had ferociously pursued all the things she'd tried not to think about when she'd been in England. She'd rented a house, spoken to her agent and to the studio. She'd done screen tests, had talked to a guy from one of the major perfume houses with the aim of being the face of a perfume she didn't wear, and had spent a lot of time talking to doctors. None of whom had been Drew.

When Carly had mentioned that she might like to slow down, she'd ignored her. Drew had given her up because of this life. If it wasn't a success, then nothing meant anything any more.

'Ready?' Carly lay on the bed in Sophie's hotel room, watching her apply her make-up and straighten her jacket.

'Think so. How do I look?'

'Businesslike and feminine. Is that what you were going for?'

Sophie laughed. 'Yes, I think so.' She was more nervous than she'd ever been. That she didn't want to show.

'Got your speech?'

'Probably.' Sophie looked in her handbag and found the sheets of paper, clipped together, right at the top. 'Yes.'

'Let's do it, then.'

Everyone had warned her that this wasn't the best idea she'd ever had. Carly first, but when Sophie had shown herself to be determined, she'd capitulated. Then her agent, who had been mollified by the studio's reaction when they'd been told. She'd chosen her charity carefully, speaking to a number of different CEOs and selecting the organisation that she felt suited her best.

Now the crunch. After a brief introduction Sophie stood up in front of two hundred people and the line of cameras ranged behind the seated guests, and went public. A concise description of her injuries and the symptoms. A slightly longer insight into the charity's aims and how it helped people with traumatic brain injury. Sophie's own heartfelt plea for better understanding and help for those who, like her, had been brain injured. And a final personal statement.

'Everyone has their own demons to face, their own difficulties. In the past months I've learned that my memories are important to me, but there's one thing that's more important. With the help and support of people I hold dear, I've learnt to define myself by who I am and not by what I can, and can't, remember. Thank you, ladies and gentlemen.'

Her legs gave way and she sat down with a bump. A moment of silence, and then applause, rippling around the room and growing until it practically deafened her. Carly leaned across, whispering in her ear.

'In other words, watch out, Josh, because we're coming to get you.'

Sophie grinned. 'We don't need to. The charity's arranged for Dr Chancellor to give an interview as a follow-up to today. I've given him permission to talk about the particulars of my case, and he says he'd like to touch on the impact those photographs had on me. I said I'd welcome that.'

'So he puts your side of the case.'

'No, he gives the facts. If they contradict what Josh has said, then so be it. I know what I think, and I believe in myself. That's what matters.'

Carly squeezed her hand. 'You've come a long way, Soph.'

If only Drew had been here to see it. The one desire of her heart that she hadn't expressed today. That would have to remain wished for ever, and silent for ever.

'Look…' Carly nodded over to where one of the reporters had for the moment ignored the news potential of the story and was clapping enthusiastically. 'That's a first. Getting a newshound to drop his pencil.'

The CEO of the charity rose, his avuncular face wreathed in smiles. He thanked Sophie, and announced that she would be available for questions this afternoon, and that after the next speaker refreshments would be available.

He offered her his arm and led her off the stage. Sophie's knees were shaking.

'I can't thank you enough, Miss Warner. We would never have been able to attract this much publicity on our own.'

'It's my pleasure. Do you have the list of papers interested in an interview this afternoon?'

The CEO nodded. 'We'll take it in your time, not theirs.' His portly, middle-aged appearance didn't remind her of Drew in any respect, but his attitude did, and that was one of the reasons she'd chosen his charity. 'Whatever you can do is a bonus. There are no expectations.'

'Thanks.' Sophie scanned the list. 'I'll see them all. Which is the most important to you?'

'This one. We've been trying to place an article with them for a long time.'

'Perhaps he'd like to join me for lunch, then.' Another name on the list had caught her eye. 'And this one. I read that paper when I lived in England.' Actually, she hadn't had much time, or inclination, for newspapers. But it had dropped through Drew's letterbox every morning.

'I'll see him for…' Sophie frowned. At the moment she was too overwhelmed to organise the list in her head.

'A chat over afternoon tea maybe?' The CEO's eyes twinkled.

'Yes, that would be good.' The adrenaline rush was beginning to subside now and she wanted to sit down.

'Leave it with me.'

'You want him to read it?' Carly was watching the CEO's retreating back with the thoughtful look that always seemed to accompany any conversation about Drew.

'I just want him to know.'

'After today, there won't be many people who don't know. But that's what you want, isn't it?'

'Yes.' The feeling of achievement was taking over from the nerves now. Steadying her, allowing her to face a long afternoon of interviews. 'It's what I want.'

Maybe it was jet-lag but Drew had found the choice slightly bewildering. At home, a rental car was just a rental car. In LA, you could rent a dream car. Whatever your dream happened to be. In the end he'd gone for a classic nineteen-fifties model with red paintwork, chrome trims and a roll back roof. If he wasn't sure how this journey was going to end, he may as well complete the last leg of it in style.

He checked out of the hotel early, unable to lie awake, working through the different possible outcomes for today any longer. He left the heavy traffic of LA behind, and the air became crisper and fresher as the road climbed and scissored, winding its way into the Hollywood Hills.

He almost drove straight past the property, which nestled among the trees, clinging tightly to the slope of the hillside. Carly had said it was a small property, and he supposed that in comparison to some of the places he'd driven past it was, but by London standards it was big enough.

Could he live here? It was quiet, beautiful, and yet you could see the morning mist covering the buzz of LA from here. Drew was under no illusions that it would be tough at first, but he could make it work.

He parked the car and walked up the steps leading to the front door. Above his head, floor-to-ceiling windows looked out onto the valley below him like blank, expressionless eyes.

Steeling his determination, he knocked. When no one answered, he wondered whether this wasn't his last opportunity to come to his senses. The trustees of the memory clinic in London had asked him to reconsider his resignation and had given him a week to get back to them.

He wouldn't change his mind. Sophie had left him a message. He knew that what she'd said in that newspaper interview was for him to read, and he wouldn't ignore it.

He got back into the car, picking up the book that lay on the seat beside him. Despite all the uncertainties, he knew he had to wait and play this thing through to the end, however long it took.

'Nice car.' Drew had deliberately stopped looking along the road, forcing his attention onto the words in front of him. When he heard Sophie's voice, the hairs on the back of his neck suddenly stood to attention.

At least it had given her some time to get her head around it. When he looked up at her, her face was composed, but her eyes were bright and alert. She was wearing trainers and running gear, holding the lead of a mid-sized, indeterminate breed of dog, which looked up at him with a great deal more interest than Sophie was showing at the moment.

'What are you doing?' She couldn't quite meet his gaze and was fiddling abstractedly with the dog's lead.

'I came to see you.'

And in the first moment he'd seen her he'd known. His decision was made. Drew knew what he wanted, and he suddenly felt that he was strong enough to move heaven and earth to get it.

Her face was still impassive. 'You'd better come in, then.'

* * *

She felt numb. Maybe that was the effect that extreme joy and extreme terror had, cancelling each other out to leave only numbness. Sophie climbed the steps to her front door and led the way upstairs to the large, open-plan living area of the house. The steeply rising ground meant that the front afforded fantastic views of the city below, and at the back there was a good-sized yard, shaded by tall palm trees.

'This is nice.' Drew glanced around, taking in the magnificent view.

'I like it.' She seized a bottle of water from the fridge and two glasses. 'Water?'

'Yes. Thanks.'

'Shall we sit outside?' She opened the patio doors, and the breeze caressed her face. This was what she'd wanted. It was what she'd planned for, even if Drew had taken matters into his own hands and forced the pace a little. Nothing could stand in their way now.

'I saw your speech. It was well done, Sophie.' His eyes softened. 'And, from what I read, it hasn't done your career any harm.'

'No. It was a calculated risk, but in the end I wanted to do it.' She ventured a question. 'You didn't come all this way to say that, did you?'

'No, I didn't. I wanted to tell you that I'm currently looking for a job.'

'What? What happened?' Her thoughts began to splinter, and she fought it. Struggled to keep it all together.

'Sophie?' He leaned forward, his gaze searching her face. 'Stay with me...'

'Give me a minute.' She closed her eyes, and took a breath. Calming herself, levelling her thoughts.

'Just breathe.'

'Yeah, I'm breathing. I'd have thought that seven years of medical training might have taught you how to recognise that.'

He laughed. 'I love it when you put me in my place, Soph.'

'Someone has to.'

She opened her eyes. 'What's all this about your job? It was such a great opportunity, and you wanted it so much. What have you done, Drew?'

'There's something I want more, Soph. I want to be with you.'

'But you can't work as a doctor here.'

'I know. I'd have to resit some of my exams. From what I hear, it might be a fairly long process, but I can do it. Medicine's my calling Sophie, but you're the woman I love. I'm putting my career on hold.'

'But… My life is not what you want.' Tears blinded her eyes. 'I'm not good enough for you.'

'That's never been true, Sophie. You're the best person I've ever met. I thought that our lives were just too different, and we could never compromise enough to be together. But we're going to have to if you love me as much as I love you.'

'Drew, you idiot. Of course I love you.' Emotion drove her to her feet and Sophie began to pace restlessly. 'I've got a flight booked to go to England in two weeks, and now you turn up here and say you've given up your job.'

He stared at her. 'But you've got a dog.'

It was a new experience to see Drew completely at a loss, saying the first thing that came into his head. 'It's Carly's dog. I'm looking after her for the week while she's on holiday. I turned the offer I had here down, because I wanted to be with you. I wanted to be the person that you could love.'

He seemed to gather his wits, getting to his feet and pulling her into his arms in one fluid movement. 'Sophie. You can't do this.'

'Why not? You did.'

Now was the only moment that mattered. Drew knew she'd need time to think about it, but he'd already made his decision. And it was only fair that she knew that. 'Sophie…'

'Yes?' She looked up at him. So beautiful. Every time he saw her the words just floated through his mind, an instinctive, unbidden reaction.

He had nothing to give her. No candlelight, no dressing up. There was at least one thing he could do. Drew fell to one knee.

'What are you doing?' He curled her arms around her waist and she struggled a little. 'Think about it, Drew.'

'I have. I'm not planning on giving up medicine, and you're not going to give up your career either.'

She quieted in his arms, perching on his knee so that he could hold her close. 'I would have. I would have come to England and been a doctor's wife…'

'That's a fine thing to be. But it's not *your* thing. We can work this out if we both give a little. There's only one thing that I won't compromise on.'

'Which is?' She wrapped her arms around his neck, her body trembling with his.

'I love you, Sophie. Please, marry me.'

'Yes.'

It was if he'd been clinically dead all these years and suddenly shocked back into life. His heart seemed to stop beating for a moment, then found its rhythm again. 'Do you need some time to think about this?'

'I've thought about it already. And my answer is yes.' She dropped a kiss onto his cheek and it was as if he'd been touched for the first time.

'You want to write that down?'

'I'll do it when I go inside. In the meantime…' she traced her finger along the line of his jaw, and Drew shivered '…we'd better start thinking about how we're going to pay the bills. Since we're both unemployed.'

'Can you go back and say you're taking the offer after all?'

'Maybe. But your job, Drew. You wanted it so much. I want it so much.'

'They said they wanted me to think about it, and go back to them in a week's time, but I said my decision wouldn't be any different.'

'Ring them. Tell them you've changed your mind.' She tried to get to her feet, almost knocking him over in the process.

'It's too early. They'll be asleep.' He held her tight, kissing her. 'Anyway, we've got something far more important to do first.'

They crossed the state line into Nevada two days later on a glittering morning. Drew was in his element. Driving a vintage car, on his way to a wedding. Their wedding. Sophie repeated the words to herself. *'Our wedding.'*

He turned to her and smiled. 'Yes, sweetheart. Our wedding. I'll be Mr Sophie Warner soon.'

'And I'll be Mrs Drew Taylor.' Sophie rehearsed the name a few times in her head.

He laughed. 'Sounds good to me. You can always keep Sophie Warner in reserve for when you want to get things done.'

She grinned at him. 'Sometimes it's useful to be able to do a bit of name-dropping.' The exquisite location, next to a waterfall. The rings, each one engraved on the inside with a promise, and the beautiful white lace dress. Everything had dropped into place, as if the world understood and blessed what they were about to do.

'I love you, Sophie.' He'd said it a hundred times, and the words still thrilled her.

'I love you too. And I trust you with everything. My life, my career.'

'And I trust you with mine.' They'd talked about it, and agreed to keep their options open but not make any final decisions yet. The one decision that they needed to make was that they wanted to be together, and that they'd both compromise to make it happen. This was no risk, no stepping into the darkness of an uncertain future and hoping things would work out. It was a step into the light.

The car sped along the highway, almost as if it too couldn't wait. Sophie consulted the map. 'We have to turn off the highway soon. We're nearly in Paradise.'

Drew chuckled. 'Nearly?'

'Yes, it's just up ahead. I want to stop at the "Welcome to Fabulous Las Vegas" sign for a photograph.'

'Another one?'

'It's a landmark. And I want a complete photographic record.'

'So you can remember who you married?'

'No.' She pulled a face at him, and he laughed. 'So I can remember how happy I am.'

EPILOGUE

DREW HAD DRIVEN all night to be with her. He parked his car in the hotel car park just as dawn broke over the harbour, and grabbed his weekend bag from the back seat.

The receptionist knew him from his previous weekend visits, and smiled at him. '*Ciao*, Dottore Taylor.'

'*Ciao*, Elena.' He took the key that she proffered and punched the lift button, smiling to himself.

The suite was in darkness, and Sophie was still asleep. Quietly he removed his clothes and slid into the warmth of the bed. She turned over, nestling against him, and Drew was suddenly entirely happy.

The last year would have been difficult to plan in advance but in practice had been the happiest of his life. Drew had negotiated a four-day week at the memory clinic, which had flourished under his guidance and hit the headlines a couple of times on account of Sophie's patronage. Sophie had landed a part in a West End theatre production, which had turned into a hit, had spent three months renovating and decorating their new home, and then two months on location on the Italian Riviera, shooting a new film.

The weekends when Drew had travelled down to see her had made the weeks without her worth it. In three weeks, when filming finished, they were going back to Vegas for their first anniversary.

'Dr Taylor.' She snuggled up against him and the long

foreplay of phone calls and an eleven-hour drive suddenly began to heat up. 'I thought you wouldn't be here until this afternoon.'

'Couldn't wait.' He slid his fingers inside the long T-shirt that she was wearing, feeling the smooth warmth of her skin.

'And I had lace, to surprise you with.'

'Lace?' He would enjoy stripping the cotton T-shirt off her every bit as much. 'I'll look forward to that tonight.'

She brushed a kiss onto his lips. 'There was something I was going to tell you.'

'Yeah? What's that.'

'Don't remember.'

He could hardly tell whether she was teasing or not. She very rarely had lapses in memory now, and she didn't let it bother her when she did.

'I dare say it'll come to you.'

'Something to do with…that.'

Yeah. She was definitely teasing. Her hand had wandered down his stomach, and her fingers brushed against the increasingly prominent evidence that he was glad to see her.

'Any more clues?' He waited, every nerve tingling.

'You and me… That discussion we had…'

Something thrilled deep inside him. 'But that was only last month…'

'I suppose you must have got it right first time.'

He rolled her over, suspending his weight above her, making sure that not an ounce of it pressed down onto her body. She giggled, aiming a play punch at his shoulder.

'I'm pregnant, not ill. You're allowed to touch me.'

'Sophie…' He'd thought that he couldn't possibly love her any more, but this moment had proved him wrong.

'Happy?'

'More than I can say, sweetheart. I love you so much.'

'I love you too.' She dropped a kiss onto her fingertips, reaching up to brush it to his mouth. 'This'll be a new adventure. You and me and a baby. I'll be at home a lot more…'

'Or I'll be at home. I'm going to insist on my right to be a great father. And a supportive husband.'

She seemed to shine with happiness. 'We'll work it out. We've done pretty well with that so far.'

He bent to kiss her. 'Yeah. Write that down, Mrs Taylor. It's a promise.'

* * * * *

MILLS & BOON®

Hardback – September 2015

ROMANCE

The Greek Commands His Mistress	Lynne Graham
A Pawn in the Playboy's Game	Cathy Williams
Bound to the Warrior King	Maisey Yates
Her Nine Month Confession	Kim Lawrence
Traded to the Desert Sheikh	Caitlin Crews
A Bride Worth Millions	Chantelle Shaw
Vows of Revenge	Dani Collins
From One Night to Wife	Rachael Thomas
Reunited by a Baby Secret	Michelle Douglas
A Wedding for the Greek Tycoon	Rebecca Winters
Beauty & Her Billionaire Boss	Barbara Wallace
Newborn on Her Doorstep	Ellie Darkins
Falling at the Surgeon's Feet	Lucy Ryder
One Night in New York	Amy Ruttan
Daredevil, Doctor...Husband?	Alison Roberts
The Doctor She'd Never Forget	Annie Claydon
Reunited...in Paris!	Sue MacKay
French Fling to Forever	Karin Baine
Claimed	Tracy Wolff
Maid for a Magnate	Jules Bennett

0815 GEN STD HB

MILLS & BOON®

Hardback – October 2015

ROMANCE

Claimed for Makarov's Baby	Sharon Kendrick
An Heir Fit for a King	Abby Green
The Wedding Night Debt	Cathy Williams
Seducing His Enemy's Daughter	Annie West
Reunited for the Billionaire's Legacy	Jennifer Hayward
Hidden in the Sheikh's Harem	Michelle Conder
Resisting the Sicilian Playboy	Amanda Cinelli
The Return of Antonides	Anne McAllister
Soldier, Hero...Husband?	Cara Colter
Falling for Mr December	Kate Hardy
The Baby Who Saved Christmas	Alison Roberts
A Proposal Worth Millions	Sophie Pembroke
The Baby of Their Dreams	Carol Marinelli
Falling for Her Reluctant Sheikh	Amalie Berlin
Hot-Shot Doc, Secret Dad	Lynne Marshall
Father for Her Newborn Baby	Lynne Marshall
His Little Christmas Miracle	Emily Forbes
Safe in the Surgeon's Arms	Molly Evans
Pursued	Tracy Wolff
A Royal Temptation	Charlene Sands

MILLS & BOON®

Large Print – October 2015

ROMANCE

The Bride Fonseca Needs	Abby Green
Sheikh's Forbidden Conquest	Chantelle Shaw
Protecting the Desert Heir	Caitlin Crews
Seduced into the Greek's World	Dani Collins
Tempted by Her Billionaire Boss	Jennifer Hayward
Married for the Prince's Convenience	Maya Blake
The Sicilian's Surprise Wife	Tara Pammi
His Unexpected Baby Bombshell	Soraya Lane
Falling for the Bridesmaid	Sophie Pembroke
A Millionaire for Cinderella	Barbara Wallace
From Paradise...to Pregnant!	Kandy Shepherd

HISTORICAL

A Mistress for Major Bartlett	Annie Burrows
The Chaperon's Seduction	Sarah Mallory
Rake Most Likely to Rebel	Bronwyn Scott
Whispers at Court	Blythe Gifford
Summer of the Viking	Michelle Styles

MEDICAL

Just One Night?	Carol Marinelli
Meant-To-Be Family	Marion Lennox
The Soldier She Could Never Forget	Tina Beckett
The Doctor's Redemption	Susan Carlisle
Wanted: Parents for a Baby!	Laura Iding
His Perfect Bride?	Louisa Heaton

three-volume *Los Vengadores de la Patagonia Trágica* (Editorial Galerna, Buenos Aires). It was published in *The Times Literary Supplement*, 31 December 1976, pp. 1635–6. In keeping with his belief in the indivisibility of fact and fiction, Chatwin resorts to the techniques of fictional narrative to relate an extravagant episode in Patagonian history.

'The Road to the Isles' is a critical review of James Pope-Hennessy's biography of Robert Louis Stevenson, published in *The Times Literary Supplement*, 25 October 1974, pp. 1195–6.

'Variations on an Idée Fixe' is a review of Konrad Lorenz's *The Year of the Greylag Goose* (Harcourt Brace Jovanovich/a Helen and Kurt Wolff book), published in the *New York Review of Books*, 6 December 1979, pp. 8–9. Later, Chatwin was to discuss Lorenz's behaviourist ideas at length in the 'Notebooks' section of *The Songlines*, presenting them as an antithesis to his own theory of nomadism.

V ART AND THE IMAGE-BREAKER

Chatwin came closest to formulating a comprehensive statement of his aesthetics when writing about the fine arts. The following texts discuss the decadence of Western art, and in doing so mark a vigorous counterpoint to the author's previous career as art expert and collector.

With its pantheon of extravagant characters, finely wrought descriptive passages and irreverent humour, 'Among the Ruins' is a characteristically 'Chatwinian' tale of modern decadence, originally published in *Vanity Fair*, April 1984, pp. 46–60, under the fuller – and more explicit – title: 'Self-Love Among the Ruins'.

'The Morality of Things', originally sub-titled 'A Talk by Bruce Chatwin', is the typescript of a speech that Chatwin gave at a Red Cross charitable art auction in 1973. It was published posthumously, in a limited private press edition, by Robert Risk (Typographeum, New Hampshire) in 1993. The text explores the philosophical and psychological implications of possession, a subject Chatwin was to return to in narrative form in his last novel, *Utz*.

BIBLIOGRAPHY

PRINCIPAL WORKS

In Patagonia, London: Jonathan Cape, 1977, 204 pp. (Paperback edition – London: Picador, 1979, 189 pp.)

The Viceroy of Ouidah, London: Jonathan Cape, 1980, 155 pp. (Paperback edition – London: Picador, 1982, 126 pp.)

On the Black Hill, London: Jonathan Cape, 1982, 284 pp. (Paperback edition – London: Picador, 1983, 249 pp.)

Patagonia Revisited (text by Bruce Chatwin and Paul Theroux; illustrations by Kyffin Williams), Salisbury: Michael Russel, 1985, 62 pp. (Reprinted by Jonathan Cape, London, 1992, 62 pp.) (U.S. edition: *Nowhere is a place: travels in Patagonia* [text by Bruce Chatwin and Paul Theroux; photographs by Jeff Gnass; introduction by Paul Theroux], San Francisco: Yolla Bolly Press book, published by Sierra Club Books, 1992, 109 pp.)

The Songlines, London: Jonathan Cape, 1987, 293 pp. (Paperback edition – London: Picador, 1988, 327 pp.)

Utz, London: Jonathan Cape, 1988, 154 pp. (Paperback edition – London: Picador, 1988, 154 pp.)

What Am I Doing Here, London: Jonathan Cape, 1989, 367 pp. (Paperback edition – London: Pan Books, 1990, 367 pp.)

Photographs and Notebooks, London: Jonathan Cape, 1993, 160 pp.

LIMITED EDITIONS, CATALOGUES AND ANTHOLOGIES

Animal Style (Art from East to West) (Bruce Chatwin with Emma Bunker & Ann Farkas), New York: The Asia Society Inc., 1970, 185 pp.[1]

Great American Families (Bruce Chatwin & various authors), New York, Times Books, 1978, 192 pp.[2]

Cobra Verde: Filmbuch (Werner Herzog). Fotografien von Beat Presser, Tagebuch von Bruce Chatwin, Gespräche mit Werner Herzog von Steff Gruber, Geschichte des Films und Dialoge von Werner Herzog. Schaffhausen: Edition Stemmle, 1987, 152 pp.

John Pawson (Bruce Chatwin & various authors; tr. fr. Spanish by E. Bonet), Spain: Gustavo Gili, 1992, 94 pp.[3]

The Morality of Things – A Talk by Bruce Chatwin, Francestown, New Hampshire: Typographeum, 1993, 26 pp.[4]

[1] Distributed by New York Graphic Society.

[2] Bruce Chatwin's contribution is entitled 'The Guggenheim Family': an article first printed in *The Times Literary Supplement* under the title 'The Guggenheim Saga'. Other contributing authors include Gore Vidal, V.S. Pritchett and Edward Jay Epstein.

[3] Part of the series 'Monographs on Contemporary Design'. Bruce Chatwin's contribution is derived from an article he wrote for *House & Garden* in June 1984, entitled 'A Place to Hang your Hat', included in the present volume.

[4] The transcript of a talk delivered by the author for the British Red Cross Society before a charity art auction held in London on 12 June 1973.

The Attractions of France, London: Colophon Press, 1993, 17pp.

Prague, edited by John and Kirsten Miller, San Francisco: Chronicle Books, 1994.[1]

PREFACES, POSTSCRIPTS, ARTICLES AND STORIES

'The Bust of Sekhmet'. In *Ivory Hammer 4: The Year at Sotheby's & Parke-Bernet 1965–66*, London: Longman, 1966, pp. 302–3.[2]

'The Nomadic Alternative'. In Emma Bunker, Bruce Chatwin & Ann Farkas, *Animal Style (Art from East to West)*, New York: The Asia Society Inc., 1970, pp. 175–183.

'Museums'. In Robert Allen & Quentin Guirdham (eds), *The London Spy – a discreet guide to the city's pleasures*, London: Blond, 1971, pp. 95–109.[3]

'The Estate of Maximilian Tod'. In Emma Tennant (ed.), *Saturday Night Reader*, London: W. H. Allen, 1979, pp. 25–37.[4]

'Foreword'. In Lorenzo Ricciardi, *The Voyage of the Mir-el-lah*, London: Collins, 1980, p. 6.

'Introduction'. In Robert Byron, *The Road to Oxiana*, London: Pan Books, 1981. pp. 9–15.[5]

[1] A collection of previously published literary works and excerpts by Havel, Kafka, Chatwin, Jirásek, Bachmann, Škvorecký.

[2] The first article known to have been published by the author.

[3] Unsigned.

[4] Also printed in the American review *Triquarterly n° 46*, Fall 1979, pp. 43–56.

[5] Reprinted in *What Am I Doing Here* under the title 'A Lament for Afghanistan', pp. 286–93.

'Howard Hodgkin'. In Michael Compton, *Howard Hodgkin's Indian Leaves*, London: Tate Gallery catalogue, 1982.[1]

'Body and Eyes'. In Robert Mapplethorpe, *Lady: Lisa Lyon*, New York: Viking Press, 1983, pp. 11–15.[2]

'Introduction'. In Osip Mandelstam, *Journey to Armenia*, London: Redstone Press, 1989, pp.4–7.

'Introduction'. In Sybil Bedford, *A Visit to Don Otavio*, London: Folio Society, 1990, pp.11–12.

CONTRIBUTIONS TO PERIODICALS

'Gone to Timbuctoo'. In *Vogue*, July 1970, pp. 20, 22, 25.[3]

'It's a Nomad Nomad Nomad NOMAD world'. In *Vogue*, December 1970, pp. 124–5.

'The Mechanics of Nomad Invasions'. In *History Today*, 22 May 1972, pp. 329–37 + bibliography, p. 382.[4]

'Surviving in Style'. In the *Sunday Times* magazine, 4 March 1973, pp. 42–54.[5]

[1] Later included in *What Am I Doing Here*, pp. 70–8. Published to accompany an exhibition held at the Tate Gallery in London from 22 September to 7 November 1982.
[2] Reprinted from the *Sunday Times* magazine: published in the UK as 'An Eye and Somebody'. In Robert Mapplethorpe, *Lady Lisa Lyon*, London: Blond & Briggs, 1983, 128 pp.
[3] Reprinted in the *Vogue Bedside Book* (edited by Jonathan Ross), London: Vermilion, 1984, 256 pp.
[4] Reprinted as 'Nomad Invasions'. In *What Am I Doing Here*, pp. 329–37.
[5] Featuring articles on Madeleine Vionnet (reprinted in *What Am I Doing Here*, pp. 86–93) and Sonia Delaunay.

'Moscow's Unofficial Art'. In the *Sunday Times* magazine, May 6 1973, pp. 36–54.[1]

'Postscript to a Thousand Pictures', the *Sunday Times* magazine, 26 August 1973, pp. 48–51.[2]

'Heavenly Horses'. In the *Sunday Times* magazine, 9 September 1973, pp. 56–61.[3]

'Fatal Journey to Marseilles – North Africans in France'. In the *Sunday Times* magazine, 6 January 1974, pp. 22–45.[4]

'The Oracle'. In the *Sunday Times* magazine, 17 March 1974, pp. 20–34.[5]

'The Witness'. In the *Sunday Times* magazine, 9 June 1974, pp. 52–9.[6]

'The Road to the Isles'. In *The Times Literary Supplement*, no. 3790, 25 October 1974, pp. 1195–6.

'Man the Aggressor'. In the *Sunday Times* magazine, 1 December 1974, pp. 28–41, 85–7.[7]

[1] Reprinted in *What Am I Doing Here* under the title 'George Costakis: The Story of an Art Collector in the Soviet Union', pp. 153–169.
[2] The postscript to a series on the history of art entitled 'One Million Years of Art' which Chatwin edited for the *Sunday Times* from 24 June to 26 August 1973.
[3] Reprinted in *What Am I Doing Here*, pp. 195–205.
[4] Reprinted in *What Am I Doing Here* under the title 'The Very Sad Story of Salah Bougrine', pp. 241–68.
[5] Reprinted in *What Am I Doing Here* under the title 'André Malraux', pp. 114–35.
[6] Chatwin's contribution to a magazine feature about occupied Paris entitled 'Life goes on'. It was later rewritten and reprinted as 'An Aesthete at War', in the *New York Review of Books*, 5 March 1981, pp. 21–5.
[7] A profile of Konrad Lorenz, excerpts of which were later included in the 'From the Notebooks' section of *The Songlines*.

'The Riddle of the Pampa'. In the *Sunday Times* magazine, 26 October 1975, pp. 52–67.[1]

'The Guggenheim Saga'. In the *Sunday Times* magazine, 23 November 1975, pp. 34–67.

'The Anarchists of Patagonia'. In *The Times Literary Supplement*, no. 3903, 31 December 1976, pp. 1635–6.

'Milk'. In *London Magazine*, August-September 1977, pp. 40–8.[2]

'Until My Blood Is Pure'. In *Bananas*, no.9, Winter 1977, pp. 10–11.

'Perils of the Israeli Settlement'. In the *Spectator*, 8 April 1978, pp. 8–9.

'Western Approaches'. In the *Radio Times*, 22 June 1978, p. 70.

'A Memory of Nadezhda Mandelstam' and 'An Introduction to Journey to Armenia'. In *Bananas*, no.11, Summer 1978, p. 5.[3]

'The Quest for the Wolf Children'. In the *Sunday Times* magazine, 30 July 1978, pp. 10–13.[4]

[1] Reprinted in *What Am I Doing Here* under the title 'Maria Reiche', pp. 94–113.
[2] A nine-page story later printed in *London Magazine Stories*. London: London Magazine Editions, 1979.
[3] Respectively reprinted as 'Nadezhda Mandelstam: A Visit' in *What Am I Doing Here*, pp. 83–5, and 'Introduction' in Osip Mandelstam, *Journey to Armenia*, London: Redstone Press, 1989, pp. 4–7.
[4] Reprinted in *What Am I Doing Here* under the title 'Shamdev: The Wolf-Boy', pp. 233–40.

'On the Road with Mrs Gandhi'. In the *Sunday Times* magazine, 27 August 1978, pp. 20–34.[1]

'Bedouins'. In *London Magazine*, November 1978, pp. 58–9.

'The Estate of Maximilian Tod'. In *Triquarterly n°46,* Fall 1979, pp. 143–56.

'Abel the Nomad'. In the *New York Review of Books*, 22 November 1979, p. 9.

'Variations on an Idée Fixe'. In the *New York Review of Books*, 6 December 1979, pp. 8–9

'An Aesthete at War'. In the *New York Review of Books*, 5 March 1981, pp. 21–5.[2]

'Von Rezzori'. In *Vogue*, May 1981, pp. 277, 328.

'Donald Evans'. In the *New York Review of Books*, 14 May 1981, pp. 14–16.

'On the Black Hill'. In *Harpers & Queen*, October 1982, pp. 164, 166, 168.[3]

'A Visit to Wiesenthal'. In the *Observer* magazine, 7 November 1982, pp. 51, 53.

'On Yeti Tracks'. In *Esquire*, 1983.

[1] Reprinted in *What Am I Doing Here*, pp. 316–40.
[2] Later included in *What Am I Doing Here* under the title 'Ernst Jünger: An Aesthete at War', pp. 297–315.
[3] Excerpts from the novel.

'Explorations of the Heart'. In *Vogue*, January 1983, pp. 220–1.[1]

'Body Building Beautiful – Lisa Lyons and Robert Mapplethorpe'. In the *Sunday Times* magazine, 17 April 1983, pp. 30–4.

'I Always Wanted to Go to Patagonia – The Making of a Writer'. In the *New York Times Book Review*, 2 August 1983, pp. 6, 34–6.

'A Coup'. In *Granta no.10: 'Travel Writing'*, Cambridge: Granta Publications Ltd, 1984, pp. 107–26.[2]

'Self-Love Among the Ruins'. In *Vanity Fair*, April 1984, pp. 46–60.

'A Place to Hang your Hat'. In *House & Garden*, June 1984, pp. 140–3.

'Great Rivers of the World: the Volga'. In the *Observer* magazine, June 1984, pp. 16–26.[3]

'Les Apocalypses'. In *Lettre Internationale*, winter 84/85, pp. 3–5.

'Where a Wayfarer Halts her Journey: A Welcoming Home for Sally, Duchess of Westminster'. In *Architectural Digest*, June 1985, pp. 202–9.

'In China, Rock's Kingdom'. In the *New York Times* magazine, 16 March 1986, section 6, part II, pp. 34–47, 104–5, 109.[4]

[1] An excerpt from *On the Black Hill*.
[2] Reprinted in *What Am I Doing Here* under the title 'A Coup – A Story', pp. 15–35.
[3] Reprinted as 'The Volga'. In *Great Rivers of the World*, London: Hodder & Stoughton, 1984. Also included in *What Am I Doing Here*, pp. 170–91.
[4] Reprinted in *What Am I Doing Here* as 'Rock's World', pp. 206–15.

'A Tower in Tuscany'. In *House & Garden*, January 1987, pp. 78–85.

'Dreamtime'. In *Granta no. 21: 'The Story-Teller'*, Cambridge: Granta Publications Ltd, Spring 1987, pp. 39–79.[1]

'The Lizard Man'. In the *New York Review of Books*, 13 August 1987, pp. 47–8.[2]

'In Natasha's Trunk'. In the *New York Review of Books*, 24 September 1987, pp. 17–18.[3]

'The Albatross'. In *Granta no. 24*, 1988, pp. 11–13.

'Chiloe'. In *Granta no. 24*, 1988, pp. 166–70.

'When the Revolution Came Home'. In *House & Garden*, January 1988, pp. 122–5.[4]

'On Location. Gone to Ghana: the making of Werner Herzog's Cobra Verde'. In *Interview*, March 1988, pp. 82–5.[5]

'Excerpts from the Songlines'. In *Aperture no.11*, Spring 1988, pp. 58–9.

'The Seventh Day – a story by Bruce Chatwin'. In *London Review of Books*, 2 June 1988, p. 13.

[1] An excerpt from *The Songlines.*
[2] An excerpt from *The Songlines.*
[3] A Review of Michael Ignatieff's novel *The Russian Album* (New York: Viking/Elisabeth Sifton Books, 1987).
[4] Reprinted in *What Am I Doing Here* under the title 'Konstantin Melnikov: Architect', pp. 105–13.
[5] Reprinted as 'Werner Herzog in Ghana' in *What Am I Doing Here*, pp. 136–49.

'The Songlines Quartet'. In the *New York Review of Books*, 19 January 1989, pp. 50–1.[1]

'Songs of a Friend for Life'. In *The Times*, 20 January 1989, p. 16.[2]

'The Bey', 'Mrs Mandelstam', 'Konstantin Melnikov: Architect', *Granta no. 26: 'Travel'*, Cambridge: Granta Publications Ltd, Spring 1989, pp. 107–25.[3]

'The Duke of M——; My Modi; The Bey'. In the *Daily Telegraph* (weekend section), 6 May 1989, pp. 1–2.[4]

'Your Father's Eyes Are Blue Again'. In the *Observer*, 7 May 1989, p. 45.[5]

'Brief Interludes'. In *Vogue*. August 1989, pp. 326–7.[6]

'On George Ortiz'. In the *New York Review of Books*, 28 September 1989, p. 62.[7]

'The Road to Ouidah'. In *Granta no. 44*, Spring 1993, pp. 223–34.[8]

[1] Excerpt from *What Am I Doing Here*.

[2] Reprinted in *What Am I Doing Here* under the title 'Kevin Volans', pp. 63–9.

[3] Excerpts from *What Am I Doing Here*.

[4] Excerpts from *What Am I Doing Here*.

[5] Excerpt from *What Am I Doing Here*.

[6] Contains the following excerpts from *What Am I Doing Here*: 'At Dinner with D. Vreeland'; 'The Duke of M——'; 'My Modi'.

[7] Excerpt from *What Am I Doing Here*.

[8] A slightly abridged version of the chapter 'The Road to Ouidah' in *Photographs and Notebooks*.

SELECTED INTERVIEWS

'Bruce Chatwin: from Patagonia to the slave trade' (with Mary Blume). In the *International Herald Tribune*, 1980, p. 7.

'In search of the giant sloth and other stories' (with Maureen Cleave). In the *Observer* magazine, 31 October 1982, pp. 32–3.

'Bruce Chatwin' (with Melvyn Bragg). In *The South Bank Show*, London Weekend Television, 7 November 1982.

'An interview with Bruce Chatwin' (with Michael Ignatieff). In *Granta no. 21: 'The Story-teller'*, Cambridge: Granta publications Ltd, Spring 1987, pp. 23–37.

'Heard Between the Songlines' (with Michael Davie). In the *Observer*, 21 June 1987, p. 18.

'Songs of the Earth' (with Lucy Hughes-Hallett). In the *London Evening Standard*, 24 June 1987, p. 33.

'Born Under a Wandering Star' (with Colin Thubron). In the *Daily Telegraph* (weekend section), 27 June 1987, p. 1.

'Bruce Chatwin' (with Michele Field). In *Publishers' Weekly*, 7 August 1987, pp. 430–1.

FILMOGRAPHY

Adaptations

On the Black Hill, by Andrew Grieve (director & scriptwriter), British Film Institute/Film Four International, 1987.

Cobra Verde (adapted from *The Viceroy of Ouidah*), directed & scripted by Werner Herzog, Werner Herzog Filmproduktion, 1990.

Utz, directed by George Sluizer & scripted by Hugh Whitemore, Viva Pictures Ltd, 1992.

Documentaries

'Nach Patagonien (Zu Bruce Chatwins Reise in ein fernes Land)', directed by Jan Schütte, Novoskop Film Jan Schütte, ZDF, 1991.

'Songlines: sur les traces de Bruce Chatwin en Australie', directed by Barbara Dickenberger, Arte, 1993.

PROFILES AND CRITICAL STUDIES OF BRUCE CHATWIN

Peter Levi, *The Light Garden of the Angel King – Journeys in Afghanistan*, London: Collins, 1972, 287 pp .

Nicholas Murray, *Bruce Chatwin*, Bridgend (Wales): Seren Books, 1993, 140 pp.

Claudine Verley (ed.), *B. Chatwin*, Poitiers: les Cahiers forell, no. 4, November 1994, 166 pp.

Alessandro Grassi and Neri Torrigiani (eds), *Bruce Chatwin: Searching for the Miraculous*, Turin: Gruppo GFT, 1995, n. p.

ACKNOWLEDGEMENTS

The editors would like to thank the following individuals and institutions for their help in the preparation of this book:

Pascal Cariss, Susannah Clapp, David Rees, Robert Risk, Francis Wyndham, Cambridge University Library, Jonathan Cape Ltd, la Bibliothèque nationale, The Bodleian Library, The British Council, The British Library, Condé Nast Publications Inc., The Library of Congress.

We are especially grateful to Elizabeth Chatwin and Gillon Aitken for reading and commenting on the manuscript.